ONE FAE IN THE GRAVE

THE PARANORMAL PI FILES - BOOK FOUR

JENNA WOLFHART

This book was produced in the UK using British English, and the setting is London. Some spelling and word usage may differ from US English.

One Fae in the Grave

Book Four in The Paranormal PI Files

Cover Design by Covers by Juan

Copyright © 2019 by Jenna Wolfhart

All rights reserved.

No part of this book may be reproduced in any form or by any electronic or mechanical means, including information storage and retrieval systems, without written permission from the author, except for the use of brief quotations in a book review.

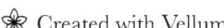

ALSO BY JENNA WOLFHART

The Paranormal PI Files
Live Fae or Die Trying
Dead Fae Walking
Bad Fae Rising
One Fae in the Grave
Book Five (Coming Soon!)

The Bone Coven Chronicles
Witch's Curse
Witch's Storm
Witch's Blade
Witch's Fury

Protectors of Magic
Wings of Stone
Carved in Stone
Bound by Stone
Shadows of Stone

Order of the Fallen

Ruinous

Nebulous

Ravenous (Coming Soon!)

Otherworld Academy

A Dance with Darkness

A Song of Shadows

A Touch of Starlight

Dark Fae Academy

A Cage of Moonlight

A Heart of Midnight

A Throne of Illusions (Coming Soon!)

1

The deep blue liquid transformed into a vivid pink while wisps of smoke curled around the glass. I set the tiny beaker onto the sleek brown surface of the bar and leaned forward as if enraptured by the overpriced cocktail. Truth was, the colour-changing drink from The Alchemist was pretty cool, but I had much more important things to worry about.

Aed, the new leader of the Fianna, had stuck around London the past couple of weeks. I'd been following him for awhile, making good use of all the boring surveillance work I'd done as a private investigator.

I flicked my eyes up from my glass and peered through the dark cloud of smoke that billowed up from Aed's drink. The fae's thick brows were furrowed over deep-set orange eyes, matching his fuzzy beard. He animatedly spoke to several other Fianna clustered around him, their strong and muscular statures matching his. It was impossible to hear what they were saying. The trendy bar was located right in the heart of the City, only a five-minute walk away from Liverpool Street Station. The post-work crowd had descended upon the place, filling it up with voices that slurred more with each passing beat.

Aed began to turn my way. Quickly, I spun on my chair and pressed my glass to my lips, drinking in the sweet pink liquid. I was pushing it, coming into the bar like this, even if I was sitting halfway across the room. It was taking a risk. If Aed saw me, he'd figure out pretty fast that I was following him. But I was getting impatient.

Fionn had been working with Nemain. That much was clear. Aed, angry about Fionn's death, had probably been caught up in her web, too.

If I could just get Aed alone, maybe I could find out what they were planning next. And prove to Balor that my loyalty was to his Court.

I spun back toward him. He stood from his stool, lifting a cigarette pack and pointing to the back section of the bar. His fellow Fianna gave a nod as he disappeared through the crowd. They stayed in place, waving over the bartender to order another round.

Bingo. This was it. The moment I'd spent weeks waiting for. This was my chance to get Aed alone and ask him some pointed questions.

I hopped off my stool, only to come face-to-face with an unsettling smile that stretched across two rows of perfect, pearly-white teeth.

"Clark Cavanaugh," Matteo said as he slid so close that his body pressed mine against the bar. "What a lovely surprise."

I blinked at him. Matteo, the leader of the

vampiric Circle of Night, looked the same as he always did. His salt white hair shone underneath the glow of the golden lamps, and his pristine pearly suit clashed against the all-black outfits worn by most in the bar. He was tall and slim, towering over my petite frame. He held up a hand and waved his adorned fingers.

"What are you doing here?" I asked through gritted teeth. My last encounter with Matteo hadn't been exactly…pleasant. That was putting it mildly. He'd thrown me into a dungeon cell and then forced me into a trial by combat in order to prove that I hadn't killed his son.

Fun times.

He arched a perfectly-manicured brow. "I see your manners have not improved."

"I really don't see the point in being pleasant to someone who tried to have me killed."

Matteo pursed his lips. "I took your side in the end. Don't forget that, Clark."

For a moment, I hesitated. That wasn't far from the truth. He'd had the option of sentencing me to death without any trial at all, and yet he'd been keen to see what happened when I fought for my life. Since then, I'd heard rumours that Thaddeus hadn't been so lucky. Still, that didn't mean I was going to become mates with the leader of the vamps.

"Is there something that you want, Matteo?" I flicked my eyes toward the Fianna. If Aed was having a smoke, I didn't have much time to get to him before he rejoined the crowd. "Because, if not, I have somewhere important to be."

The twinkle in his eye dimmed just the slightest.

"My people tell me that you are no longer a member of the Crimson Court. Is that true?"

Something sharp and pointy stabbed at my heart, and I had to take a deep breath in through my nose to keep my body steady. Even though I understood why Balor had kicked me out, it still hurt like hell. And not just because I missed my Prince, the warmth of him, the scent of him, the feel of his hands on my skin. I missed it all. Moira, Elise, Kyle, even Duncan. I missed my tiny little room. I missed waking up at the arsecrack of dawn to join my team in the command station. Prepping for missions, laughing over stacks of pizza boxes.

I blinked back tears, and suddenly, my face felt very, very hot.

"I see," Matteo said quietly, without waiting for my response. I supposed he could see the answer in the watery sheen in my eyes. "I fear Balor has made a mistake with that."

"He had his reasons," I said.

"So I heard," Matteo replied.

"Is that all?" I asked, casting another glance at the cluster of Fianna. "Because I really have somewhere I need to be."

"Yes," Matteo said slowly, arching a brow. "How interesting that you are here when the Fianna are as well. You're still fighting Balor's battles for him even when he's banished you away from his side."

With a roll of my eye, I pushed past Matteo, shaking his words out of my ears. Vampires. They really could be bloody annoying at times.

I pushed through the crowd, my shoulders jostling against arms and bags and drinks, until I reached the back section of the bar. Two open doors led to a garden terrace sandwiched in the crevices of closely-packed buildings. Aed was just putting out his cigarette, tossing it onto the ground and crushing it beneath his heel.

I stepped up beside him just as he turned to go back inside.

His hand fell to his side, eyes flickering with a mixture of interest and wariness. Aed towered over me. If I were to guess, I'd put him at being at least six foot two. Maybe more. His muscles strained against the tight black shirt hidden underneath a leather jacket. But that wasn't all he hid underneath there. He'd have a dagger, or some other kind of weapon. Just because I couldn't see it didn't mean it wasn't there.

"You look familiar," he said in a lilting Irish accent. "Have we met before, love?"

I arched a brow. Well, this certainly made things easier. I'd mistakenly assumed he'd recognise me straight away. When he'd stormed into the Throne Room a few weeks ago, I'd been there, standing by Balor's side.

"No, I don't think we've ever been properly introduced."

The warmth in his eyes vanished, the twin orange flames going hard. My American accent must have tipped him off. Slowly, I could see the puzzle pieces coming together in his mind. He pressed his lips together, and his hand shifted closer to his jacket on his left side. That would be where the weapon was then.

"You're Balor's new fae. The psychic one."

I tried to stop the pain from flickering across my face. "You're right, and you're wrong. I'm the psychic one, but I'm not Balor's."

He didn't bother to ask what I meant by that. He most likely knew. He'd been attempting to spy on the Crimson Court as much as I'd been spying on him. Granted, he wasn't as good at needling out information, but he would have most likely heard what went down between me and Balor. It wasn't exactly a secret in the London supernatural world.

His eyes narrowed. "What are you doing here then? Trying to weasel yourself into another House? Well, you're barking up the wrong tree, Clark. My House is technically part of Balor's Court, even if we're mostly independent. We couldn't let you through the front doors. Even if we wanted to."

Hmm, that was interesting. The final bit. Not any of the stuff that came before it. It confirmed a suspicion I'd had from the moment I first saw the Fianna sneaking around the Crimson Court's building late into the night. Aed no longer wanted to be a part of Balor's Court.

"You're working with Nemain, aren't you?"

Aed stiffened. That was confirmation enough by itself, but I needed to hear confirmation with my own (mind's) ears. Sucking in a deep breath, I plunged my magic forward. I pushed against Aed's mental boundaries, finding the slightest boundary to protect his thoughts from fae like me. It was weak, almost as though he'd only recently learned how to put up the wall. It only took a few hard shoves before I could plow right through.

Aed's mind was a jumble. Thoughts flew by, whipping about like a frenzy of fears and hopes and dreams. Words echoed all around me. It made no sense, not without context. That was the problem with reading minds. It wasn't as simple as knowing every single thought that flitted through a person's head. It was about finding the right thought. And it was about directing the mind toward the information that was needed.

Nemain warned me about this.

Ah, so there it was. Quickly, I pulled back out of his head.

"Good," I said with a smile. "Now that we understand each other, I need you to tell me exactly what she's planning to do next. And don't act like it's nothing. She's been coming up with plan after plan after plan. So far they've all failed. But she'll have something else up her sleeve. What is it?"

Aed just blinked, and then snorted out a laugh. "What's it to you? You're not part of his Court anymore, Clark. Go find something else to do with your life. Go home."

Home. My heart squeezed tight. What was my home? It wasn't America, the place I'd fled when my grandmother had sent me away to stay safe. Sure, it was where I'd been born. It was where I'd grown up. But I had never felt at peace there. I'd always been waiting for the other shoe to drop. Home wasn't my tiny little flat in East London either. It had been a roof over my head and a bed for my tired body, but never a home.

Home was Balor's Court.

"You know what?" I asked, glad that my voice came out far steadier than I'd expected. "You're right.

I *will* go home. Just as soon as you tell me what Nemain plans to do to Balor next."

Before he had a chance to answer, I dove straight back into his head again. This time, his thoughts were clearer, and it didn't take long for me to hear exactly what I'd come to find.

She better go back to where she came from, or Nemain will curse her, too.

I sucked in a sharp breath and pulled out of Aed's head, my ears ringing. "A curse? What kind of curse? What has she done, Aed?"

He shook his head and began to back away. "Your power comes straight from the Underworld. It isn't natural. Get out of my damn head."

"I'll stop reading your mind if you tell me what it is I want to know."

He ground his teeth together, his eyes flashing. I could tell he was considering it. One thing I'd quickly learned over the years? People hated it when someone dug through their thoughts. It was a violation, one that was way worse than a punch to the face. Hell, even I understood that, though I was willing to do it to get the information I needed. I'd been so scared all these years of running into another psychic that I hadn't even dared allow myself to even think about my own secrets, for fear of someone finding out.

Mainly, that I had unwittingly helped my parents (well, my mother and my step-father) kill Balor Beimnech's sister, so that Nemain could take the Silver Court's throne.

Hence, why I was currently banished from walking through the Crimson Court's front doors.

"You know what?" he said in a low growl. "Fine.

I'll tell you what I know, and then you need to get the hell out of here."

I crossed my arms over my chest and lifted my chin. "Spill it then."

He sucked in a deep breath, and then let it out so slowly that I thought he might be going into some kind of trance. Finally, he spoke. "Nemain went to one of the ancient cursing stones and managed to get it to work. She used it against House Beimnech. They're all going to die, most likely within a few days. They're cursed to end up in the grave."

2

It took a few moments for Aed's words to fully sink into my mind. Of all the things I'd expected him to say, this certainly hadn't been it. My heart pounded hard; my palms went slick with sweat. It was all I could do to keep myself standing upright. Nemain had done far worse than I'd feared. She'd cursed everyone I knew and loved to die. Within days.

This couldn't be happening.

"See?" Aed arched his eyebrows and smirked. "I told you that you'd be better off going home. Now, scurry on out of here and leave me the hell alone."

Aed twisted on his heels and stomped back into the bar. Heart hammering hard, I followed after him. He may have told me what Nemain had done, but that wasn't good enough. I needed details. Anything that could help me figure out a way to make this right. This was no longer about me getting in good with Balor again. All of their lives were in danger.

I reached out and wrapped my hand around Aed's

thick bicep. He whirled toward me, his orange eyes flashing with anger. "Get out of here, Clark. We had a deal."

"I need to know more about this cursing stone. Where is it? How did she get it to work? Is there a way to undo the curse?"

He ripped his arm out of my grip. "I don't know any of that. All I know is that it's done. Within the week, Nemain will sit on that throne made out of skulls, and there's nothing you can do to stop it."

My heart thumped hard. Aed had confirmed the nightmare I'd heard inside his mind. Everyone would be dead within a week.

"You must know more than that," I said, desperate for some kind of tidbit that could lead the Court to safety. "Anything at all. How she did this. How to undo it. Where and when and what."

"I want nothing to do with this," he said in a low growl. "Balor made a terrible mistake, and now he's going to pay for it. He never should have harmed Fionn. He never should have driven Tiarnan away from us. He may be our Prince, but that does not give him free reign to be cruel."

I ground my teeth together. "Fionn tried to overthrow him. He set Balor up, got him arrested by the human cops. Tiarnan helped him. And then Fionn took the throne, but not before sentencing me to die. Tell me, Aed. Was Fionn right in what he did? How would you have responded if he'd done all that against you? If he'd sentenced someone you care about to die?"

Aed pressed his lips together. "Balor must not care

all that much about you if he banished you from Court."

Pain shot through my gut. That one hurt. That one really hit hard.

I stepped up closer to Aed, lifted my chin. "Don't make this personal."

"Or what?" Aed sneered. "You going to take out every Fianna leader who doesn't perform according to your standards? Because I hate to tell it to you, love, but the Fianna live by their own rules, for their own people. We might be a part of the Crimson Court, but we answer to ourselves."

"For now," I said. "Keep pushing things, and I doubt you'll have your independence for long."

He let out a low chuckle. "You're on the losing side in this, love. Nemain is going to win. And then she's going to end this shit alliance with shifters, vampires, and fae. But you wouldn't want that, would you? Not with that filthy blood running through your veins."

Okay, I'd heard enough.

I stabbed my finger into Aed's rock hard chest. "Tell me what you know. *Now*."

"You don't want to fight me. And I don't want to fight you. You're a tiny, little thing. I'd only break you."

"Underestimate me all you want. That'll only make it all the more satisfying when I kick your ass."

Aed's hand drifted down to his side and rested on his sword. I quirked a smile and did the same. For what felt like a century, we stood there on the outdoor patio of The Alchemist bar, staring each other down, threats shooting out of our eyeballs. I was waiting for him to make the first move, but he was doing the same for me. If I wanted to get this show on the road, I was going to have to do something drastic.

Like swing my sword at his head in the middle of all these humans.

That probably wouldn't go over very well with the staff.

"Come on," Aed finally said in a low voice. "Walk away from this. I have no beef with you, and you shouldn't have any beef with me."

"Give me the information, and I'll walk away."

He narrowed his eyes.

"Fine."

I dove back into his head. It was a risk, leaving my body when Aed could draw his sword at any moment. But I wasn't going to leave here without knowing everything I possibly could about what Nemain had planned. His mind was thick with rage, his thoughts churning at a million miles an hour.

This little shit has no idea what's coming for her. If she finds the Bullaun that cursed everyone, it will undo the spell. But she'll never find it. Nemain made sure it was hidden well. Even I don't know where it is.

I pulled out of his head, satisfaction pounding through my veins. I'd gotten what I came for, even if it wasn't much to go on for now. It would have to be enough.

A scream ripped through the night. Whirling, I turned with my hand pressed to the top of my hilt. Several humans were clustered together, waving at Aed and I. Their eyes were open wide. Fear was plastered across their faces.

"She has a sword! She's one of those dangerous fae!"

I let my hand drift from my sword. "No, I'm really not. I swear I'd never hurt you. I—"

But it was too late. The humans had begun to flee the bar, and in the chaos, Aed was gone.

3

I yanked up the garage door and plunged into darkness. In the dimly-lit space, I spotted Ronan lounging on his sofa, watching a sportsball game on a tiny television set in the corner. Ronan, with his shoulder-length hair and rugged beard, had become my, er, *roommate* of sorts when I'd been kicked out of the Crimson Court. We had kept things strictly platonic over the past couple of weeks, despite the tension that literally peppered the air whenever we came within twenty meters of each other.

He arched a brow and stood, his rumpled black t-shirt hiking up to show the ridges of his six pack abs. Normally, I would blush and glance away, but I was far too angry to worry about how desire coiled in my gut. Instead, I let myself just stare.

"Hard night at the office?" he asked, his voice dripping with sarcasm. Ronan had let it be known that he did not approve of my desperate attempt to get back into Balor's good graces.

"You could say that." A beat passed. "Do we have any gin?"

"We have beer." Ronan crossed the room, opened the tiny refrigerator door, grabbed a beer, and then tossed it my way. I caught the cool can without even thinking, my arm moving with an instinctual speed.

Ronan's lips quirked. "Your reflexes have gotten damn good, Clark."

"Yeah, well." I brushed off the compliment. "None of that matters. Not when everything is going to literal shit."

He crossed his arms and leaned back against the dingy wall. "What happened? Wait, don't tell me. You spotted Balor cosying up with a random brunette at his club."

I scowled. Truth was, in my days spent stalking, er, surveilling, I had seen Balor come and go to his club several times, a habit he'd seemingly broken when I'd been a member of his Court. But he was back to his old tricks again, a development that was getting underneath my skin, despite the fact I knew he wasn't taking girls to his bed.

He couldn't and wouldn't, or else he risked siring the bastard that would one day stab him in the face. According to the prophecy, anyway.

Anyway, none of that was important. Not now.

"I finally got Aed alone," I said, popping the tab of the beer. Quickly, I took a long gulp of the bitter beverage. I was more of a gin girl than a beer girl, but I was glad for the cool liquid, even if it wasn't my first choice. "Turns out I was right. Nemain had another plan. This one is worse than the others."

"Let me guess." Ronan grabbed a beer for himself,

and then crossed the room to stand before me. He clinked his can against mine. "She's trying to raise another army of the dead."

"I wish," I said.

"How could it be worse than a mindless army that will do whatever it takes to kill who she demands?"

"Because there's no need for an army, Ronan. There's no need for her to do anything at all now."

Ronan tucked his finger underneath my chin and forced me to gaze up at him. A shiver went through me, that strange electrifying yearning he always brought out of me. "Stop talking in riddles. Tell me what's going on."

"She's cursed them all to die within days."

He was quiet for a moment, his eyes flashing. Then, he let go of my chin and stepped back. "Okay. I see what you mean now. Balor needs to know immediately."

I frowned. "There's no way he'll agree to see me."

"You don't need to see him, Clark. I'll go. He knows you're staying here with me, but I doubt he'll turn me away."

I took a sip of the beer and stalked over to the cage where Ronan sometimes stayed if he worried his wolf might get too out of control during a shift. "I need to tell the Court myself. And I need to find a way to reverse whatever it is that Nemain did."

A beat passed in silence. "And did Aed tell you how to do that?"

"No," I said, tightening my grip on the beer can. "He doesn't even know where the cursing stone is, much less anything about the magic that it wields. I'm going to have to find someone else who knows how it works. It's the only way to stop everyone in my Court from dying."

"Clark," Ronan said in a low growl that made goosebumps pop up all over my skin. But I knew what that tone of voice meant. He'd used it several times these past few weeks. "We should make sure Balor knows about this, but that's all you can do. That's all you *should* do. I don't understand why you're so determined to put your life on the line after he banished you the way he did. It's not your Court anymore."

I whirled toward Ronan, tears pricking my eyes. "Because I care about them. They're going to die, Ronan. All of them. Even if they're not my Court anymore, I can't just let them end up in the grave."

"That's why I will tell them about it. And then they'll be able to find a way to reverse the magic themselves. They have far more resources for that than we do."

"I want to help them. I want them to know that I—"

He let out a heavy sigh and shook his head. "And see, that's what this all goes back to, your need to prove your worth."

"And what's wrong with that?"

"Anyone who has ever met you knows exactly what you're worth, Clark Cavanaugh," Ronan said, using the surname I'd chosen for myself instead of the one my step-father had tried to give me. "Your step-father used his power on you, to manipulate you into doing his bidding. Balor knows it, too. He's seen what you've done for his Court. He's seen exactly how loyal you are to his cause. You don't need to prove yourself. If anything, he needs to prove *himself* to *you* after banishing you the way he did."

He set down his beer can, crossed the room, and took mine out of my shaking hands. Leaning forward, he grasped my fingers in his and tugged me closer to his chest. He placed the tips of my fingers against his beating hard. "You don't need to prove yourself to me. I see exactly who you are. I can give you things that he would never be willing to share."

I blinked, staring up into his dark eyes. The raven within me cawed. It recognised Ronan for who and what he was. A shifter, like me. Someone who was willing to accept me, warts and all.

Shuddering, I leaned against him, but a part of me could not stop thinking about the one male in the world I needed to forget. Balor. His flickering orange eye. His strong hands. His power and magic, and the way it felt when he curled it around my body.

I pushed those thoughts away.

"You seem cold," Ronan murmured the words against my ear.

In fact, I was shivering. My teeth chattered as the warmth of my body escaped from me.

"Have you been shifting again?" he asked, rubbing his strong hands up and down my back.

I gave a nod. Any chance I got, I shifted. I transformed into the bird and back, so many times that I barely had to think about the stages of anger and desire that it took in order to get me there. The only problem was, too many repeated shifts often left me weak and cold.

"You need to take a break sometimes," he said, moving away to grab a thick blanket from the sofa. He hadn't even owned a duvet before I'd moved in, but now the place was covered in blankets, pillows, and cosy sheets. "You're incredibly powerful, Clark, but you're not invincible. It will take your body a little while to get accustomed to its new abilities."

I took the blanket with a soft smile and wrapped it around my shaking shoulders. "I know. I'm just eager to get to where you are with your shifting."

"Hell, you're practically there already, Clark. My recovery time is just less than yours."

"They're not really new abilities though, are they?" I asked. "I mean, I was born with them. It's not like they just came out of nowhere."

"You may have been born with them, but you hadn't used them until a few weeks ago. Give it time. You've already made massive improvements in such a short time." He sucked in a deep breath. "To be honest, I've never seen anyone else come into their shifting powers quite like you have. It's almost like…"

"Almost like what?" I asked.

He shook his head. "Nothing. It will sound crazy if I say it."

I frowned. "Well, now you *have* to say it."

He waited a moment before he spoke again. "It's almost as if your transformation into the raven comes from more than just your latent shifting powers. It sometimes feels as though it's coming from your fae side as well."

I blinked at him. "That doesn't make any sense."

"See?" He laughed. "Like I said, it sounds crazy. What's far more likely is that your dad was badass. It's a shame you can't talk to him about all this."

I fell silent. I didn't want to talk about my father,

or even think of him. It hurt far too much for me to go there. Instead, I stepped up closer to Ronan and wrapped myself up in his arms, my eyelids growing heavy from the warmth of his body and the blanket.

"Let's get you some rest so that you can recover from your shifts," he said in a gruff voice. Slowly, he peeled off my clothes, and then his, letting the heat of his body seep through my skin. Desire sparked within me, but we'd long since drawn lines between what we could and couldn't do. I wasn't ready to get involved with someone else, and strangely, he'd respected that far more than I thought he would.

And so I merely fell asleep in his arms.

4

I slid out of Ronan's arms, crept across the floor, and pulled my shirt back over my head. Despite my stealthy moves, I felt more than heard him rustling from behind me. When I turned back toward him, he stared up at me through one cracked-open eye.

"You're going to him." His voice was flat, emotionless.

"I'm going to Moira." I pulled on a black leather boot, and then grabbed the second from the floor. "They need to know what's coming for them. Balor will refuse to see me, but Moira won't."

Sighing, Ronan pushed up onto his elbow. His expression still held no emotion, but I could tell that he wasn't happy about my decision to continue on with my mission. "I'm sure that he has forbidden Moira and Elise from speaking to you. He may have even used the Princely bond."

"Yeah, well." I shoved my foot into the boot. "I'll do all the talking. Moira just has to listen."

As I stalked toward the warehouse door, I stopped to grab my sword from where I kept it propped up in the corner.

"If you're really determined to do this, I won't try to stop you," Ronan said quietly. "But I will suggest you don't take that weapon onto Balor's property. Talking to his fae is one thing. Storming into his Court with a sword after he's banished you?"

Ronan was right. If I wanted them to listen to me, I needed to appear as non-threatening as possible. So, I left both him and my sword behind.

Surveillance had always been the most boring aspect of my work as a private investigator. Even with mind reading powers, sitting and watching was one traditional part of the job I couldn't avoid. The best way to get through the mind-numbing hours was to grab some snacks and power through with the radio down low. During my two weeks away from the Court, I'd commandeered an old junky car that could barely make it across four city roads before it threatened to break down. But it did what it needed to do, which was provide me with a vantage point.

I sat on the ripped leather seat with an open bag of pick-n-mix on my lap, peering through a set of binoculars I'd liberated from a box of my old stuff that Balor had allowed Moira to deliver to Ronan's warehouse.

Through them, I could see that the Court was very quiet tonight. Much quieter than it had been in recent days. After I'd left, there had been a lot of activity.

Guards coming and going, Balor pacing across the front stoop with his furrowed brows pinching the space between his eyes. He and the guards had been on some kind of mission. Being left out of it had been another punch to my already beat-up heart.

After several hours of this, one o'clock struck on a distant clock. The single chime rang out in time with the widening of the front door. Tossing a sour chew into my mouth, I rolled down the window to get a clearer view. Duncan, Moira, and Cormac streamed out onto the stoop, their expressions animated as they turned toward…

Balor stepped out onto the landing. My stomach flipped over itself a thousand times. I had only seen him twice during my surveillance missions, both toward the beginning of my banishment from his Court. It had only been weeks, but it felt like years. All my thoughts and emotions slammed into me like a train, punching me so hard that it felt as though I could barely breathe.

He looked the same as he always did. His dark hair was shot through with silver streaks, and the patch across his eye hid his boiling red iris from view. The power of him rippled across the distance, and everything within me arched toward him. My heart ached. My stomach boiled. It almost felt as though a piece of me was missing, and that piece was standing right there. But still out of reach.

It took me a moment to remember why I was here, what I was doing, and what I needed to do.

Balor was cursed. He was destined to die if I didn't figure out a way to stop it.

With a deep breath, I cracked open my door and

stepped out of the car. Shielding my eyes from the nearby streetlamp, I continued to watch Balor and his guards on the front stoop of the Crimson Court's headquarters. It was a majestic building, a multi-million dollar purchase that had required millions more to transform it from the rundown, abandoned Battersea Power Station into what it was now: a home for all of the fae in London.

After several moments of animated discussion, the guards went their separate ways. Balor went back inside with Duncan while Moira began a routine check around the property. In about ten minutes, she'd pass the bushes on the right edge, where I'd be waiting for her. Time to make my move.

~

"Hi, Moira." My voice was softer than I intended, and it hitched up on the final syllable of my friend's name. At least, I hoped she was still my friend. We'd parted on good terms. She didn't blame me the way Balor had, but it had been weeks since we'd last spoken. Her feelings toward me could have changed. She could have hardened against me.

I wouldn't even blame her if she had.

She whirled toward me with her high golden ponytail slashing through the air, and her breath caught when her eyes landed on my shadowy form in the bushes. "Fucking hell, Clark. You scared me half to death. What the hell are you doing lurking in the bushes like that?"

Everything within me relaxed at the tone of her

voice, relief pouring through me. There was no anger there, no hardness. I stepped out of the bushes, though being careful to keep myself hidden in the shadows.

"I'm sorry to creep up on you like this, but I really need to talk to you about something."

She grinned, stepped forward, and wrapped her arms around my neck. "You have no idea how glad I am to see you. I was worried you'd left London."

I squeezed her back. "I could never leave London. It wouldn't let me, even if I tried."

She let out a light laugh, pulled back, and scanned my face. "As glad as I am to see you, Balor's going to lose his shit if he sees you on the premises."

"I know." I bit my lip, glanced down. "I'm surprised he didn't forbid you from speaking to me, to be honest."

"He did." Moira shrugged when I jerked my head back up. "He just didn't use his bond to stop us from disobeying him."

I'd expected him to do this. It wasn't a surprise. When a fae got banished from a Court, it was usually for good reason, and Balor had one. Not only had I helped kill his sister, but I'd helped install a murderous fae into power. And now, she was going after Balor's Court, too. She'd had his fae murdered. She'd conspired against him. She'd found a way to curse them all to die. Of course he wouldn't want anyone within his Court to speak to me.

That didn't change the fact it hurt that he'd gone that far.

A part of me had hoped he wouldn't.

Moira shot a quick glance over her shoulder. "Nevermind that. We should hurry. I'm supposed to be meeting Duncan and Cormac in the next half hour. If I show up late, they'll know something is up." And neither Duncan or Cormac would be as quite as understanding as Moira about my presence here. "Is something going on?"

I pressed my lips together. "So, I don't even know how to tell you this without freaking you out, so I might as well just spill it."

With a deep breath, I told Moira everything I knew. Which wasn't much, to be honest. As I explained, the smile drifted from her face until her lips had hardened into a tense, straight line. Her face had even blanched white, transforming her into the stoic warrior she was.

"Are you certain of this?" she asked in a grave voice. "Aed wasn't lying to you?"

"I read his mind to confirm."

Moira swore underneath her breath. "And he didn't give away how to reverse this?"

"He didn't know. Nemain likely kept that information to herself."

A deep, rumbling voice broke out from behind me, making me jump ten feet in the air. Power washed across the lawn. A familiar power. One that I yearned for every waking moment of my life.

"Clark."

I twisted to face my former Prince, every cell in my body bouncing with a desire to jump off my skin. He towered before me, his face blotting out the moon. Shadows curled around his body, dancing off of him as he strode my way.

"Er, I think I'll be going now," Moira said quickly.

"Good idea," Balor said in a low growl. "I need to deal with Clark myself."

5

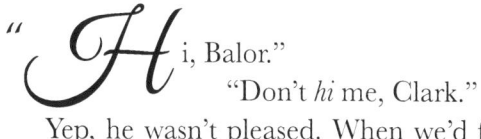

"Hi, Balor."

"Don't *hi* me, Clark."

Yep, he wasn't pleased. When we'd first met, he'd used this tone of voice with me, especially when he wanted to get his point across. Cold and distant, full of anger and power and threat. Over the weeks that I'd come to know him, that tone had dropped away to reveal something else, something much softer in him. He wasn't the terrorising fae his reputation might suggest. He cared deeply about his Court, about every fae within it. And he'd come to care for me.

That anger, that coldness, that threat, it was meant for those on the outside of his carefully constructed world.

And now I was on the outside.

I swallowed hard, ignoring the tight squeeze of my heart. "I'm not sure what else I'm supposed to say."

He narrowed his single orange-red eye, one that looked as though flames resided within it. I was all too aware of how true that really was. I'd seen Balor burn things down on more than one occasion. Buildings, enemies, other fae. They had always been enemies, those outside of his circle of protection. And now I was, too.

"You're supposed to say nothing. You're not even supposed to be here." Balor rolled back his shoulders, power rippling off his body in waves. "Don't pretend you don't know what a banishment means. Normally, you wouldn't even be allowed to stay in London. Now, go back to Ronan. Before anyone else sees you, and I'm forced to do something we'll both regret."

My heart thumped hard. "Are you threatening me?"

"Clark." Balor ground his teeth together, making the lines of his jaw ripple. Once, I had kissed that jaw. I had felt that mouth on my skin. It had only been for a moment. Such a fleeting instance in time, but it replayed in my mind in full technicolour when everything else around me was muted in shades of grey. "I had to send you away. I had no other choice, even if I had wanted to keep you in the Court. Everyone knows who you are now, what you did to contribute to Nemain's power. There are some who expected me to take your head and add it to my collection of crimson skulls. A banishment is getting off lightly."

Frustration began to roil through me. All this time, I had been beating myself up about my past. What I'd done had been a horrible thing, and I would do anything in the world to take it back. But Moira's words kept echoing in my ears, more and more as the days went on. I had been manipulated by my stepfather. Those hadn't been my actions, not really. He'd used his power on me to get me to do what he wanted.

I had not killed Balor's sister.

As if sensing my thoughts, Balor gave a grim nod. "Yes, I realise that you were not the mastermind behind the attack and that you are not the one to blame for what happened. If you were…I would not be being so polite to you right now."

I arched a brow. "This is you being polite?"

That red eye narrowed again. "You cannot come here again, Clark. Please don't make this harder than it needs to be."

"I'm not the one making this hard, Balor," I said, my voice almost coming out a whisper. He winced as I took a step closer to him and placed my trembling palms on his chest. Everything within me shuddered at the contact. It had only been weeks since we'd last touched, but it felt like years. The familiar feel of his strong abs and sculpted pecs made every cell inside my body ache with the kind of need I'd only ever felt around him.

I wanted to curl up against him. I wanted to wrap my arms around him and pull him close. I wanted nothing else between us ever again. No horrible curses from the past. No prophecies destined to keep us apart forever. No vampires, no Sluagh, nothing.

Balor shuddered, his body betraying him. He leaned against my touch, sucking a deep breath in through his nose as if he were breathing in my scent. "I can smell your need."

One of Balor's many gifts was the ability to sniff out emotions, and mine right now were practically bouncing off of me. I wondered if he smelled the same way I did. I wondered if I had the same effect on him as he had on me. If only I could read his mind…I could find out. But he was one of the only beings in this world whose thoughts evaded me like whispers of wind through my fingers.

"I can hear yours," I whispered.

His eye slightly widened. "I thought you were unable to hear my thoughts. My mental barriers are very much in place. You shouldn't be able to hear a damn thing."

"I can't," I said. "But I can still hear it anyway. Or maybe it's more that I can *see* it, regardless of what you want me to think you feel."

"Clark." His expression darkened. "We can't do this. I've made my decision. You are banished from the Crimson Court. That means you cannot come near here. You cannot interact with my fae. And I certainly cannot be seen speaking to you."

"Yeah. Heaven forbid you're seen talking to the fae who has tried to save all your asses on numerous occasions. Don't forget that if it wasn't for me and my bird friends, your alliance with the vampires would be broken right about now."

His jaw rippled as he ground his teeth together, and then he glanced away. "What you have done to help us does not matter, not when everyone knows the truth about your past."

"Fine," I said. "I get it. I'm banished. I'm not welcome here. And I have to get the fuck away from you. Doesn't matter. I didn't come here to try and get you to forgive me."

His eyebrows winged upwards. "Then, why have you come here, Clark?"

I sucked in a deep breath. "There has been a…

development. One I thought you'd want to be aware of."

Twin lines appeared between his eyes as his expression hardened. "What kind of development?"

"So, I saw Aed tonight. You know, the angry Fianna who took over from Fionn?" I left out the bit about the whole burning Fionn to a crisp thing. I had a feeling that would only irritate him more, not that it felt possible at the moment. Balor was peak irritation at this point.

"Even though House Futrail and I have had our differences recently, they are still an official part of the Crimson Court." His lips set into a thin line. "That means you cannot speak to them either, Clark. You're to stay away. From all of us."

"Tough shit," I snapped. "Because House Futrail has been working with Nemain. And you want to know what she's up to? Because I know. If it didn't mean the deaths of pretty much every member of your House, then I'd be inclined to turn around and walk away from you right now, with the way you're speaking to me."

His single red eye drank me in, the ferocity in his expression impossible to ignore. Heat crept up my neck, in spite of every attempt I made to hide the desire I felt for him. "What do you mean?"

"I think I'm right when I assume you know what a cursing stone is?"

"A Bullaun?" He lifted a brow. "Of course I do. I'm surprised you do, however. It has been decades since they have been around."

"Apparently not. Nemain got ahold of one. And she used it."

Darkness flickered in his orange eye. "Tell me everything you know."

So, I did. It wasn't much, but it was enough that he now knew the severity of the threat. But when I finished explaining what I'd learned, the darkness in his eyes had completely disappeared.

"You don't look concerned," I said with a frown.

He gave a quick shake of his head. "I know what you've been doing these past couple of weeks, Clark. You've been keeping an eye on me, but I've also been keeping an eye on you. You've been trying to find a way to get back in my good graces."

I pressed my lips together, cheeks reddening.

"You don't deny it?" he asked.

"No," I said, figuring honesty was the best policy, especially after everything that had happened between us. Hiding things from Balor was what had gotten me into this mess in the first place. "I've been following Aed, so that I could find out Nemain's plans. I thought that if I brought them to you, then you'd forgive me and let me back into the Court."

The tension in his shoulders hardened his upper body into a stiff piece of stone. "And you have not been particularly successful in cornering Aed."

"Not until tonight."

"The cursing stones no longer exist, Clark. Not like they once did," he said in a low, dangerous voice. "They haven't for a very long time. You've either made this up after coming up empty, or Aed was lying to you about them."

My eyes widened as I took an unsteady step back. "You don't honestly believe I'd make up a story about a curse? Not when it affects every single member of your House?"

"I wouldn't have believed it before," he said quietly.

Before he'd found out the truth about my past. Before he knew that I was the daughter of murderers. Before all the trust and love we'd built between us had been ripped to shreds and tossed on the ground. Pain coiled around my heart, squeezing tight like a venomous snake.

"I am not making this up. Nemain has cursed your House. You have to believe me."

"I don't have to do anything of the sort." Balor took a step away from me. "Now, go home, Clark. Go back to Ronan."

"That is not my home," I said, voice cracking. "My home is in your Court. But that's not even what matters to me right now. What matters is making sure everyone in your House is safe. You'll all die, Balor. Elise, Moira, Kyle, you. Please don't walk away from this just because of your anger toward me."

But it was no use. Balor Beimnech had made his mind up about Clark Cavanaugh. There was no talking him out of his hatred toward me, the distrust he felt about every word that came out of my mouth.

Balor sucked in a deep breath, spun on his heels, and walked away from me.

6

*B*alor left me standing in the middle of the footpath, alone and frustrated that I couldn't make him understand. For a moment, it had felt like we'd made some steps back to how things had been between us before. Even though I couldn't read his mind, his emotions had betrayed him. He wanted to forget about what had happened. He wanted us to move past it.

But he couldn't. He was the Prince. There were things expected of him, and one of those things was not forgiving a McCann. Nothing I could say would change his mind. I knew I could be stubborn sometimes, but he could be, too.

With a deep breath, I spun on my heels to head back to the warehouse where I knew Ronan would give me a lovely "I told you so" lecture. And I tried to tell myself that would be just fine. I had come here to do what I sought out to do. I had warned Balor. Now, it was up to him. The problem was in his hands. I had done my best to prove to him that I was on the Court's side.

And he'd given me a warning. I really was to stay away from now on. If I didn't, he'd made it clear that he would no longer to continue to hold back on the punishment that Faerie would demand if I kept throwing his banishment right back into his face.

I squeezed my eyes tight as the sound of the rippling water of the Thames rose up around me. Walking away now? That just wasn't me. I could no sooner ignore the threat on Balor's life than I could turn my nose up at a slice of pizza. My former Prince might not want to believe the threat was real, but that didn't mean it wasn't.

And if he wasn't going to look into it, then he was practically forcing me to ignore his order.

He'd given me no other choice.

I had to find out how to reverse the curse.

A woman stepped out of the shadows and onto the footpath before me. For a moment, nothing registered. She looked almost human, a thick woollen hat tucked over her long brunette hair. She was tall and slender, an expensive maroon coat fitting her body like a glove. Only her eyes gleamed, bright and dark at the same time. It was impossible to tell what colour they were. They were almost like pools of shifting sand.

And that was when it hit me. I had only seen eyes like that once before.

The woman from the shadows was Nemain.

My heart thumped hard in my chest. Nemain was here, in London. The fae responsible for all of the attacks against Balor and his crown. It was all I could

ONE FAE IN THE GRAVE

do not to stumble back, but I held my ground. I'd only met this fae a handful of times, but the truth of her was writ full in my memories. She was larger than life, a monster from my childhood who had once stood ten feet tall in my mind.

She quirked a smile, lips painted a dark red that matched her coat. "I heard a rumour you were here in Balor's Court, but I didn't want to believe it until I saw it for myself. Hell, I thought you were dead. Balor's men killed your mother and your step-father. I thought he'd had you killed, too."

Blood roared in my ears as I stared hard at Nemain, my mind barely comprehending her words. "What?"

I was off to such a great start. In my dreams, I had imagined punching the monster from my childhood right in her tiny, perky nose the moment I next laid eyes on her. Instead, I felt—and probably looked—like a bumbling idiot.

She arched a brow, one that had been clearly drawn on for maximum dramatic effect. "You mean, you don't know? He never told you? Oh, dear."

Finally, her snarky tone of voice snapped me out of my stupor. "Stop speaking in riddles and explain yourself, or I will draw my sword."

She laughed. "You don't have a sword, darling."

I glanced down. Shit. I'd left my sword back at Ronan's place as a way to show Balor that I didn't want to come across as a threat. I was unarmed.

"But have no fear, I am more than happy to explain what I meant." Her smile widened. "When Balor learned his sister had been killed, he dispatched some of his men to assassinate the….well, the assassinators, really. They went above and beyond, those men of Balor. They not only killed your parents, but they went after the rest of your family, too. Including you and your grandmother, though I can see now that part wasn't true. Did Balor know you survived?"

The world had slowed to a stop. All the noises of the city had been drowned out by Nemain's words. She had to be lying. There was no way that Balor was behind the deaths of my parents, the reason I'd had to go on the run and into hiding all my life.

But…it made sense in a way that twisted my gut. It was no secret that Balor could be violent when necessary, and he would have considered this necessary. It had been his sister. He would have been wrecked by pain and sorrow. He would have wanted the murderers dead.

But it still shook me that it had been him. He might not have swung the sword, but he'd passed the sentence. If it weren't for the wit of my grandmother, I would be dead right now because of him.

"So, I was right. You didn't know. I suppose he left that part out when he banished you from his Court."

"Just stop," I said through gritted teeth. "I've heard enough."

She sniffed at the air. "Don't tell me that you still feel beholden to him somehow. He's banished you from his Court. Your bond is broken."

But it didn't feel as though our bond was broken at all. I felt just as consumed by Balor as I always had, maybe even more so.

"Whatever. Your little curse thing isn't going to

work." Nemain's churning eyes slightly widened, giving me a flicker of satisfaction. "Yeah, that's right. I know about your curse. And I'm going to be the one to end it."

"That's a shame," she said, twisting her lips back into a smile. "Because I was just coming here to make you an offer. You helped me get my Silver Court crown. You helped put me on that throne. You can help me take the rest of them, and you will be handsomely rewarded if you do. A position of power, one that most fae can only dream of."

I narrowed my eyes. "The rest of them? You don't honestly believe that you're going to be able to take control of every throne in the world, do you? All seven of them?"

"Oh, I most certainly do."

So, this was worse than I thought. Nemain not only planned to take Balor's throne, but she was going to go after the other five as well. There were seven total Courts in the world, though that hadn't always been the case. The Courts ebbed and flowed with the division of continents, along with humanity. The Bronze Court covered all of the Middle East while the Emerald Court included all of Asia. The Sapphire Court was South America, the Ivory Court was Africa, and the Onyx Court Australia and New Zealand. Antarctica didn't have a Court. It was one of the only free lands in the world, along with a handful of islands.

"Good luck with that," I said with a scowl. "You might have weaselled your way onto one throne, but you'll never get the rest. Not even Balor's, despite how many times you try. You will keep failing. And I will always be there, making sure that you do."

She let out a heavy sigh that sounded far more sarcastic than truly defeated. "Have it your way. After what Balor has done to you, you would be smart to choose the winning side. But you are more your father than your mother. I see that now."

Anger boiled within me. How dare she speak about my father.

And then she drew her sword. Steel sliced through the air, ringing loud in my ears. Moonlight glinted off the blade, slipping down to the carved hilt. The hilt was wood and gold combined, the carving smoothed down as if from decades of use. It was impossible to tell what it had once been, though two furrowed eyes were clear.

"Run, fight, or join me," Nemain said in a voice as steely as her sword. "Your choice, Clark McCann."

"It's Cavanaugh," I said, raising my fists up before me, begging my body to remember the moves that Balor had once tried to train into me.

Her teeth glittered as she smiled. "Fight it is then."

Her blade swung toward me before I knew that it was coming. Just in time, I ducked down, and I heard the steel sing as it passed over my head. Taking a deep breath, I flattened myself on the ground and swung out my leg. My foot connected with hers, and she stumbled sideways.

For a split second, I had time to think. I was not going to be able to beat her, not as long as she held a weapon. I'd grown faster and stronger since embracing both the fae and shifter sides of my life. I could fight well. But not that well.

And if I ran now, I had no doubt that she would most likely catch me.

I had to fly.

Taking a deep breath, I let my deepest and darkest emotions flood into my mind. I focused on the pain I'd felt when Balor had turned away from me. I felt the rage that came along with Nemain's presence here in London, from her words, from the knowledge that Balor had been behind the attack on my family, even the innocents.

It didn't take long for the shifter within me to awaken. My body began to transform, my limbs crying out in pain as feathers sprouted along my arms. My vision went bright; new scents flooded my mind. The ground fell away beneath me as my wings flapped against the air, taking me high into the sky away from Nemain.

She stared up at me, triumph flickering across her face. But there was also something else there. A hint of concern. A question-mark in her eyes. Had she never seen a half-fae shift before? I knew there were more like me out there, those with parents who were both of the fae and shifter, though we weren't exactly common. Fae and shifters didn't like to mix much. Hell, Nemain forbade it of her Court members. Shifters and vamps were the enemies, not friends. It was one of the reasons why her Court was so at odds with ours.

Ours.

I still looked at the Crimson Court as though it were mine. When it was anything but.

Pain tore through me at the thought. Soaring through the air, the world around me began to dim just as a hundred ravens circled my shifted form. They cawed and swooped, surrounding me.

And then the world dimmed into nothing but murky shadows. Shadows so thick I couldn't see anything but mountains upon mountains of grey.

7

Ouch.

My whole body hurt, especially my head. I cracked open my eyes and stared up at the dark sky above me. The moon was bulbous and bright, almost bright enough to hurt my eyes. Groaning, I pressed a hand to my head and tried to make sense of the past few hours.

Or had it been hours? It was hard to say. Normally when I shifted, I blacked out immediately. Tonight was the first time I'd actually seen the world as my bird. And, usually, a long time passed before I shifted back.

This felt like it had only been an hour. Two, at most.

I pried my eyes open even wider and pushed up, glancing around.

Holy shit.

One of the many Morrigan statues stood tall before me, her shadow stretching down the courtyard path. I was *inside the Crimson Court*. A bench sat empty to my right while the glowing windows of the west wing of the building rose up high on my left. I was smack dab in the middle of the path with moonlight glowing down on top of me. It would only take one fae glancing out of one of the many windows, and I'd be spotted within a heartbeat.

Still wincing from the pain, I crawled into the shadows of a nearby bush and cursed my raven beneath my breath. My raven was me, of course, but right now she felt like a traitor that lived inside my own body. She'd known I wanted nothing more than to be back inside of the Crimson Court, and so she had soared over the rooftops and deposited me here.

If Balor found me, he would be…incensed, to say the least.

But if another fae found me, it would be even worse. He'd made it clear that some of them thought I should be dead.

So, this was going to be fun.

Taking a deep breath, I scanned my surroundings. As was typical at night, the courtyard was empty. No one was out here. So, all I would have to do was sneak inside the building and out the front door.

No big deal.

Right?

Out of the corner of my eye, I could have sworn the Morrigan statue shifted from one looming form to the next. I jerked my head toward it, half-expecting for the entire stone thing to have moved down the pathway. But all was still. It looked just as it had moments ago. This Morrigan had been stunning. Tall but not lithe. Her shoulders were strong, her arms etched with muscles. I recognised her as Morrigan IV, the fae who had led her kin on the ancient battlefield against the Ivory Court, back when there were a mere three Courts instead of seven.

Her side had won, of course. It was both a blessing and a curse of The Morrigan. Whatever side she joined always won. But, sometimes, the Morrigan chose the wrong fae to back.

"Do you think you can get me out of here alive?" I whispered up to the statue.

"Emma said she saw Balor and Clark talking on the front lawn," a soft voice drifted to me.

At first, I could have sworn it came from The Morrigan, but then two female fae drifted into view from the opposite end of the courtyard.

I recognised them both, but I was pretty sure I'd never spoken a word to either of them. Or them to me. After I had joined the Court, I had always been so busy. I'd only ever had the time to get to know my fellow guards. It had been guard duty twenty-four seven. And when it wasn't guard duty, it was Balor.

"I can't believe he's talking to her," another one of the females said. She had long dark hair and olive skin, and her eyelashes looked as long as my arm. "I mean, why the hell even bother to banish her if he's just going to ignore his own rules?"

The original girl snorted. "They had a thing. Didn't you know that? Clark was seen coming and going from his penthouse all the time. Plus, he went to her room, too. They were totally fucking."

"Balor wouldn't sleep with one of his own subjects," the dark-haired beauty said. "He never has. Doesn't want to make things complicated."

"Well, he sure as hell changed his mind on that

one," she chirped. "It's like a whole star-crossed lovers thing now."

I needed to get out of here. For one, they were getting closer and closer to my hiding spot inside of the bushes. And two, well...I really didn't want to squat here like a lunatic, listening in on them talking about my love life. Or the lack thereof. I hadn't been aware that the entire Court apparently thought Balor and I were sleeping together, and I kind of wanted to press rewind and shove that fun tidbit out of my head.

Slowly, I crept through the thick bushes, edging closer and closer to the back door of the building. But the voices just kept following.

"You know what I think?" the original girl said. "I think he only banished her for show. They're totally still doing it. They just have to hide it from everyone else."

"But she's a McCann," the dark-haired girl said. "Her family killed the Princess. And she hid it from him. No way in hell he'd have sex with her after finding that out. Not to mention, how can he trust her? She's probably working with Nemain."

Irritation boiled inside of me. Balor had been right. Everyone in the Court thought the worst of me. They didn't understand that I'd been manipulated into doing my step-father's orders. They had no idea how much pain and fear Nemain had thrown into my life.

They thought I was guilty. They thought I deserved the punishment I'd gotten. Or worse.

The girls passed by my hiding spot without noticing me lurking in the bushes, and strode toward the door that would lead them back into the building.

Pulling the cool night air into my lungs, I pushed

up from the ground and slid inside the building, just behind the gossiping girls. I made it inside just in time, kicking out my foot as they continued striding down the corridor, with no idea that their supposed enemy had slithered into their midst.

Now, I could go right and head straight out of the building. I would probably never see it again after this. My trip to the Court tonight had made my status as a solitary fae clearer than ever. Balor would never give in, and his Court wouldn't either.

I was an outcast. I was unwanted. I was the enemy.

But, despite all that, I couldn't leave them here to die.

So, instead of getting the hell out of this place, I turned my body left and inched down the corridor to the wide sweeping staircase that would take me up to the second floor.

The Court was quiet this late at night, all the fae tucked in their rooms until morning. In House Beimnech, every member had their own unique room with floor to ceiling windows looking out at the London skyline. Because of the large number of us—*them*, now—the rooms weren't much bigger than a standard bedroom. But the amenities were much nicer. All needs were catered for. There was no need to leave the House for anything, not if you didn't want to. There was even a restaurant on the premises that boasted of three Michelin stars.

Need a new toothbrush? Balor could get it delivered. Yes, fae even cared about brushing their teeth. We might not have to worry about cavities, but having nice breath was a plus.

At the bottom of the stairs, I couldn't help but pause and glance in the direction of Balor's office down the rear corridor. I'd spent many evenings in there with him, pow wows and plotting, sharing drinks and stories from our past. Just never too much of the past, of course. I'd always held back from him, even after he'd made it clear I could trust him with anything.

With a heavy sigh, I dragged myself up the stairs. He might not want to listen to me, but his second-in-command might. Elise and I had almost grown as close as I had to Moira. We'd been a trio of terror for Balor. A triple pain in his ass.

No one in the Court knew, except for a handful of us, that Balor had named Elise as his second to take over the Court in case anything happened to him. A lot of the fae thought he'd given that distinction to Duncan. It wasn't a terrible assumption. Duncan was one of the strongest fighters in the entire Court. He was always the first to be chosen to go on dangerous missions. And Balor confided in him more than most.

But Elise was smart. And she'd stood by Balor's side for a very long time. Duncan might be the better choice for battle. But Elise was the right choice to lead.

I reached the top landing, and another pang went through my heart at the familiar corridor that stretched out before me. I had paced this hall every morning and every night for weeks. Even though I had only been a part of the Court for a short while, this stretch of carpet had been etched firmly into my mind. I knew it like the back of my hand, which was why it took mere seconds for me to find myself standing before Elise's room.

With a deep breath, I knocked on Elise's door, glancing to the right and to the left. There were cameras mounted in the corners. Kyle was likely watching.

The door cracked open. Elise's pixie face stared out at me. A million emotions flickered through her silver eyes until her expression finally settled on what I hoped was relief. And then she opened the door wider, welcoming me inside.

8

"What are you doing here?" Elise hissed as she grabbed me and pulled me into her room. Moira was leaning against the wall by the window, arms crossed over her chest and looking not the slightest bit surprised.

She gave me a wry smile. "Told you she'd make it. Time to pay up, Elise."

Elise swore under her breath, pulled five pounds out of her pocket, and shoved it into Moira's open palm.

My eyebrows shot to the top of my forehead. "You were seriously betting on whether or not I'd come save your asses or not?"

"No, we both know you'd try to come," Elise replied with a rueful smile. "We just weren't sure if you'd make it past Balor the grumpface."

"He really has been grumpface since you've been gone," Moira added.

"I mean, he *tried* to stop me," I said before shrugging. "Okay, he did stop me. I was going to go back to

Ronan's. And then I had a change of heart when Nemain showed up spouting shite."

"Whoa, wait a minute." Moira pushed off the wall and crossed the room, coming to stand before me with furrowed brows. "Please tell me we're still in banter mode and you're not serious."

"I am afraid I am deadly serious, Moira. After Balor gave me his lecture, Nemain showed up and tried to talk me into joining her insane mission to take control of the seven Courts. When I said no, she tried to fight me. So, I flew off. When I woke up, I was in the courtyard."

It was a lot of information to throw at them at once, but they took it in stride.

"Sounds like your shifter training has been coming along nicely," Moira said.

Elise shot her a look full of horror. "We just found out Nemain is an egomaniac, and you're focused on Clark's ability to shift?"

"We already know Nemain's an egomaniac. It's not really a surprise that she wants to take over all the Courts, is it? Hell, at this point, I'd be more surprised if she didn't."

"She has to be stopped," Elise whispered.

"You're right. She does." I frowned at Moira. "You haven't told Elise about the stone thingy, have you?"

"Er, no." Moira found it within herself to actually look a bit ashamed. "Balor forbade me to say a word, and he used his bond on me this time. I tried to tell her, but…well, you know how it goes."

Balor and his damn Princely magic.

Frowning, I crossed my arms. "I hate it when he

uses his bond magic almost as much as I hate it when he uses that damn allure."

Elise cocked her head, frowned. "As much as I'm dying to know what you guys are talking about, what do you mean about Balor's allure?"

"You know." I shrugged. "It's his third power or whatever. He can cast an allure, and it makes people act like idiots around him. He basically can make you want him."

Moira snorted, and Elise grinned.

"What?" I demanded.

"That is not one of his powers, Clark," Moira said.

"No, it definitely is."

"Nope," Elise chirped. "I've known Balor a long, long time. I know all about his powers, his gifts. He's super powerful, and there's a lot he can do. Allure? That's not one of them."

My cheeks filled with heat. All this time, I'd been convinced that part of my draw toward Balor had to do with his allure. What I often felt around him wasn't logical. It wasn't normal. He had been casting his power toward me, making me react in a way that I never would.

It couldn't have all been real.

There was no way in hell that it was normal.

Elise's eyes flickered as she smiled. "Maybe you two really are mates."

I didn't want to hear it, not after the past few hours. Not only had he pushed me away once again, but I'd learned that he was responsible for the deaths of all my family. And not just my mother and my stepfather, two deaths I could understand after what they'd done. But my entire family, including innocents, had been destroyed.

I blinked away the tears and tried to focus. "Enough about Balor. We need to talk about the curse."

"Curse?" Elise flicked her eyes toward Moira, who gave a grim nod.

"Clark will have to tell you. I'm forbidden from saying a word."

And so I did. Taking a deep breath, I started from the beginning. My plan to follow Aed until he gave me what I needed. The run-in where I discovered just how far Nemain was willing to go to get what she wanted, up until the moment she'd approached me outside of the Court. By the time I was done with my story, Elise's face had turned ashen. As Balor's second, she had a lot of power of her own to wield, especially if Balor hadn't specifically commanded her otherwise.

And, thankfully, she seemed to be taking this a lot more seriously than he was.

"Okay, this is bad," Elise said, wringing her hands as she paced from one end of the small, dorm-sized room to the other. "This is really bad. Balor really doesn't want to do anything about this?"

"He doesn't believe me," I said. "He thinks I'm spouting bullshit. Either to trick him in Nemain's name or to make up ways to get back into his good graces. I'm not sure if he's decided whether or not I'm working for the enemy."

Elise frowned. "He's stubborn, but I think he knows deep down that you're not the enemy some people think you might be. Unfortunately, we just don't have the time for him to come around to this on his own."

"So, what do you propose we do?" I asked.

"I'm not sure yet, but we have to do something. Maybe Kyle or Duncan will have an idea."

Grimacing, I swivelled toward Moira, whose face was a reflection of the same unease I felt. "You don't think Duncan will go straight to Balor the *second* I step foot inside the command station?"

Kyle, we might be able to convince. He'd always been kind to me, and the two of us had developed a kinship during our time spent working together. Duncan, on the other hand, had never quite warmed up to me the way the others had. Grudgingly, he'd come to accept me as a member of the team. Now that I was officially banished and not a member of said team? No way in hell he'd going along with me being around.

"I don't think we have any other choice," Elise said, striding to the door and yanking it open. She motioned forward with a meaningful look. Completely no-nonsense.

Moira and I exchanged a glance.

"I guess we know where Elise stands on the issue."

Moira cracked a grin, and then motioned for me to go first. I took a deep breath and stepped outside into the hall. Immediately, dread pooled in my gut. I could sense him. My former Prince. He was somewhere down the hallway, and he was coming straight toward us. And fast.

Quickly, I turned back to the door and motioned for Elise to open it again, hissing as I spoke. "Balor is coming. I need to hide."

Elise stepped forward and placed a hand on my shoulder, her silver eyes twinkling. "Don't worry. He won't see you."

A strange sensation flooded through my body. A sensation I'd only felt once before, the day I'd joined the Crimson Court. Elise had been the one to cause that feeling then, and she was doing it again now. She had cast a glamour over me.

"Just don't say anything," she whispered. "Your accent will give you away."

I pressed my lips together, spine as stiff and straight as a London lamp post. Just as I'd braced myself for impact, Balor rounded the corner from the western end of the corridor. He was all scowls and narrowed eyes as soon as he spotted the three of us hovering outside of Elise's room. On either side of me, I heard my friends take in a lungful of air.

"Moira." Balor frowned as his eyes scanned from Moira, to Elise, and then to me. "Elise. Who is your friend here? She's not a member of this Court."

"This is…Alyssa. She's a member of the Pack and wanted a tour of the premises. I figured since we're allies and all…well, why not, right?"

Balor's gaze hadn't left my face as Elise had fumbled through her lies. I wondered what Balor could smell, if he could smell anything, coming from Elise. He had the ability to sniff emotions, but could he scent out fibs? I hoped for all our sakes, he couldn't.

"Alyssa," Balor repeated. "Does that mean you're a wolf shifter? You're pretty small for that."

Elise's glamour, while impressive, was limited in some aspects. She could completely change someone's face, as well as body shape. What she couldn't do was make someone appear taller—or shorter. So, Balor was now looking down at a very familiar five foot two.

I cleared my throat, desperately trying to avoid speaking aloud.

"Not a wolf," Elise said quickly. "She's a fox."

Balor's frown deepened. "Since when did the wolves welcome foxes into their Pack?"

His single red eye pierced into me. The meaning of his tone of voice was clear. He wanted me to answer the question, and if I lobbed it onto someone else again, I would only raise his suspicions even more. Which begged the question…did he suspect that I wasn't Alyssa? Balor wasn't stupid. Plus, there was that whole scent thing. He hadn't made any suggestion that he thought I was Clark, but the intensity of his gaze suggested that he didn't totally buy what we were selling.

"The Pack has a close relationship with—" Elise began, before Balor cut her off.

"Alyssa can answer the question," he said quietly.

I cleared my throat again, my cheeks growing hot. And then I took a deep breath, putting on my best (which was to say it was terrible) British accent. "Like Elise explained, the Pack are close mates with a few of the city foxes. We aren't officially members of that lovely society, but we socialise quite often. With spots of tea. Cheerio, govna."

Cheerio?! Govna?!

Mentally, I smacked myself in the head. In my effort to sound as British as possible, I'd gone and ruined it by throwing ancient slang in there that no one ever used. Slang, I must add, that made absolutely no sense in the context I'd used it.

For a moment, I couldn't breathe. Balor stared at me, his face so expressionless that it looked as though it had been carved from stone. My heart beat madly in my chest. I was certain his face would turn red with rage. I was sure he would collect me, throw me over his shoulder, and then toss me out on the steps. Or into the dungeon. And then he'd do the same to Elise and Moira for socialising with the enemy and lying to him about it.

But, instead, his lips quirked. "Cheerio, govna. Enjoy your tour."

And then he drifted off down the corridor, as if nothing strange at all had just happened.

I twisted toward Elise and hissed. "What the hell just happened?"

She looked just as dumbfounded as I felt. "I have no idea. Did Balor the smiter just say, 'Cheerio, govna'?!"

"Yes. Unless I am hallucinating. Which I might very well be," Moira said, blankly staring down the corridor in the direction that Balor had disappeared. "How did that not tip him off that it's you?"

"I don't know," I said. "But we can't stick around and wait for him to come to his senses. We have a curse we have to break."

9

The command station was exactly the same as it had been when I'd left it. Full of power and steel and echoing footsteps. We strode inside and stopped just before a round oak table that squatted in the center of the expansive space, cluttered with maps and police reports. Duncan and Cormac were nowhere to be seen, thank the seven. I did not look forward to explaining to them why a shifter fox was lurking in their most secure of spaces.

Kyle was in his ever-present spot behind a bank of computers, however. His curly red hair fell down into his eyes, and his tongue was stuck out between thin lips. On his messy desk cluttered with soda cans and old pizza boxes sat a single flourishing plant—a cactus my old friend, Ondine, had given to him.

He glanced up, and his eyes widened when he saw me (still glamoured) sandwiched between Moira and Elise. "You shouldn't have brought her here."

"This is Alyssa," Elise began. "She's a shifter, and we're giving her a tour of the Court."

"Don't bother," Kyle said with a wave of his hand. "I have access to all of the security cameras at all times, remember? I know everything that's happened tonight."

I didn't really know how to reply to that. And neither, it seemed, did Elise and Moira. Instead, we all stood there awkwardly by the planning table, mouths glued shut.

At least I wouldn't have to try and speak in a British accent again.

"Are you going to report us?" Elise finally asked, her voice quiet.

Kyle grabbed a soda can and popped the tab, running his other hand through his brilliant red hair. "I should. Our Prince made it more than clear that our friend here is not welcome on the premises. That said, something is clearly wrong if you're all going to this much trouble to get her into the command station. I'm willing to hear you out before I call in the calvary."

I let out a long, slow breath in relief, and then we all filled Kyle in on what had happened. By this point, I'd told the story so many times that I pretty much had it memorised.

"A cursing stone?" Kyle asked with a frown. "It's been a long time since anyone has used one of those. It was thought that they didn't even work anymore."

"So, you know about the cursing stones?" I asked, moving over to stand by Kyle's desk. I propped one hip on the top of it, just as I had done countless of times when I'd been a member of the Court. The move was so familiar, so easy, so right that another pang of pain went through my heart. I missed this. All of this.

Being in the command station talking strategy with my closest friends in the world…it was the only life I wanted.

Kyle spun in his chair, a frown affixed to his boyish face. "I don't know as much as I'd like. They're incredibly old, and they were thought to be dead, so there hasn't been much focus on them at all for at least two hundred years."

Moira let out a low whistle. "Two hundred years? Damn."

"That's a long time," I added.

"Not in fae years," Kyle reminded. "For some, like Balor, the time of the cursing stones won't feel that long ago at all."

We all looked at each other. Like me, Kyle was a newbie fae. He'd been born not long before me. Moira was older, but she was still less than a century. Elise was the oldest—a one-hundred-and-fifty year old fae who had seen a lot in her time on this earth. Still, none of us were as old as Duncan, Balor, or even Nemain. They had been a part of this world for a very long time.

"Do you think we should try to ask him about them?" I asked.

All three of my friends gave me a frank look.

"Okay, not *we*. Someone else." I glanced to Elise. "What if you just casually brought it up? You could say that you overheard some of the girls chatting about the cursing stones in the courtyard."

"He's not an idiot, Clark."

"Well, we need to find out about them somehow." I turned back to Kyle. "Do you think you can find much using your fancy, albeit creepy, hacking skills?"

Kyle snorted. "I could use my hacking skills, or I could just…Google it."

I rolled my eyes. "Okay, smart-ass. Get to it then."

Kyle tapped on the keyboard, sticking his tongue out between his teeth. After a moment, several images popped up on the screen, photographs taken of moss-covered stones mixed in with crude drawings. There were about six of them in total. Too many. We didn't have time to run around the world searching for cursing stones.

"It looks like half of them are in this country," Kyle said, glancing up at me. "The other half are in unknown locations. I think the knowledge of where they are has been lost over the years."

"So, there are three potentials here," I said with a frown. "We don't have time for that."

"Three is better than six," Elise said chirpily.

"One would be ideal," I said. "Aed seemed to think the curse would only take days to kick in. That's not much time to track them all down."

"Luckily," Kyle said after a few more taps on the keyboard, "one of the stones is here in London."

My ears pricked up, and I leaned forward to stare down at the image Kyle had displayed on his state-of-the-art screen. There wasn't much to look at, just a slab of stone covered by more stones.

"London?" I asked. "I mean, Nemain's in London now. Maybe she came here specifically to use this thing."

"Makes sense to me," Moira said with a nod.

"From the looks of it," Kyle continued, "there are no stones in America."

"So, she had to come here," I said with a nod.

"Excuse me. You can't be in here," Duncan's booming voice sounded from behind us. In unison, we all whirled toward the entrance of the command station. The leader of the pack stood in the doorway, filling the entire frame with his massive bulk. He glared at the four of us, his hands curled into fists by his sides. "Moira. Elise. I thought you knew better than to bring a stranger into our command station."

Well, shit. I was going to have to put on that bloody accent again.

Elise's face paled as she tried a smile. "This is Clarissa. She's a visitor from the Pack. Balor said we could give her a tour of the grounds."

"Alyssa," Moira hissed in a low voice.

Elise's face scrunched up in confusion.

"Well, which one is it then?" Duncan asked as he crossed his beefy arms over his chest.

"Erm, it's Clarissa Alyssa. Lovely home you have here, innit." A strange grin spread across my face, one that I was certain made me look deranged.

Duncan looked like he bought this whole thing just as much as I bought that he was perfectly happy to defer to Elise on all matters revolving around the Court.

"Yeah, alright. Clarissa Alyssa." His expression darkened. "I don't bloody well care if you have permission to go on a tour of the premises, you can't be in here. Authorised personnel only."

"I authorised her," Elise said. "She is a member of the Pack, who are our allies. We're working together with them to ensure the safety of all supernatural London."

"Balor hasn't mentioned anything about this," he said.

"That's because I'm the point of contact for this," she said breezily. "I don't know why he would have decided to mention it to you."

Elise was doing her best to pull this off, but Duncan still did not seem convinced. It likely wasn't every day that Balor kept important information hidden from him. If the guard team truly had brought in a shifter ally, Duncan would have been involved in the situation.

"Look, Elise," Duncan said. "Something just doesn't seem right about all of this."

"Well, you're welcome to go and bother our Prince about it if you'd like. Even though he's busy. Super busy."

I held my breath in my throat. Elise was throwing her best bluff out there. Hopefully, Duncan would fall for it.

"You know what?" He took a step back. "You're right. I think I *will* go take it up with him. If anything, it'll remind him that I should always be aware of any visitors we have coming into this Court. The safety of the fae depends on it. Meanwhile...don't show her anything confidential, eh?"

And with that, Duncan disappeared out of the command station, his feet turned in the direction of Balor's office.

As soon as he was out of earshot, I turned to my friends with a hiss. "Shit's about to hit the fan. As soon as Duncan asks Balor about the shifter in the command station, he's going to figure out pretty quickly that I'm me."

"No kidding," Moira said. "We need to get you out of here."

But I'd only just arrived. I wasn't ready to leave yet. We'd barely had time to gather info about the cursing stone, let alone come up with a solid plan on how we were going to attack this thing. The world had started to feel right again. Moira and Elise on either side of me. Kyle at the bank of computers.

I didn't want it to end.

"Come on." Moira grabbed my arm and pulled me out of the command station, hurrying alongside me to the front exit. I still had on my glamour, but my skin pulsed against the magic as if the real Clark would break through at any moment.

Somewhere in the distance, I heard the unmistakable rumble of Balor's voice, and the gruff, clipped words of Duncan. Footsteps sounded on the floor. The door was only a few meters ahead. We needed to make it. We had to move fast. But with every step, another part of my soul felt as though it was chipped away.

Moira yanked open the door and cast a quick glance over her shoulder. "You've gotta go. They're coming."

"Moira." I hesitated, unable to find the words I wanted to say.

"Don't." She gave a fierce shake of her head. "This isn't goodbye. We'll see each other soon.

And, just as Balor's familiar figure rounded the corner down the hallway, Moira shut the door of the Crimson Court in my face.

10

"Let me guess. You need my help with something." Ronan was outside of his warehouse when I returned back "home." He stood hunkered over an old beat-up motorcycle that he'd bought off a random buy-and-sell Facebook group, and he'd spent the past few days fixing it up. He cranked the engine, smiling when it sparked to life. All it needed was a fresh coat of paint now, and it would be good as new.

"The fae of London need your help."

He gave me a look.

"Which means that I need your help."

"And Balor actually asked this of you?" He'd phrased it as a question, but he'd spoken it more like a statement than anything else. He knew Balor hadn't asked me to do a damn thing.

"Admittedly, he doesn't know I'm helping." I strode forward and ran a hand down the rusted exterior of the bike. "Scratch that. He knows I'm *trying* to help. But he may have told me to leave things the hell alone or else."

Ronan let out a rough chuckle, tossing a wrench next to his toolbox. "And so you decided that meant you should *not* leave things the hell alone."

"He didn't believe me about the curse. If he's not going to do anything about it, then I don't see another choice."

"Alright then." Ronan crossed his arms over his muscular chest. "So you want to save the fae."

"I do."

"Alright. I'm not going to argue with you. It's pointless to, anyway. You're stubborn as hell. Besides, Balor is the only thing holding the supernaturals of London together. I don't really want to imagine what would happen if he died."

"And I need your help. Moira and Elise are booked in for guard duty tonight, so they can't get away without raising suspicion."

He arched a brow. " I'm not sure I like the sound of that. I suppose you have a plan?"

"Of course I have a plan. But I have to warn you, it may or may not result in intense pain."

Chuckling, he threw up his hands. "This is why I don't like roommates."

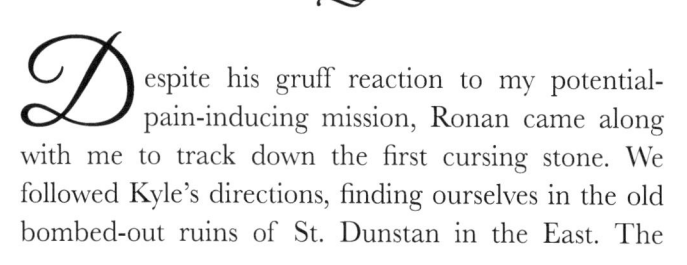

Despite his gruff reaction to my potential-pain-inducing mission, Ronan came along with me to track down the first cursing stone. We followed Kyle's directions, finding ourselves in the old bombed-out ruins of St. Dunstan in the East. The pocket of the past was situated in the center of the finance-heavy City. Named after a tenth-century monk involved in black magic, leprosy, and the Devil, the church had long been rumoured to be the site of ghosts or dark powers or creatures from the mists.

During the daytime, it's a pocket of green amidst all the steel and stone. But, at night, like right now, it was dark and full of shadows. Trees shot through broken windows; vines wound themselves around crumbling stone walls. Shadowy archways cast whispers through the silence, beckoning us to step through their looming doors. Doors that I could only imagine led to something insanely creepy. Even though the dark magic and demons were ancient lore, something likely imagined by superstitious humans, I swore I could feel magic humming beneath the very ground on which we stood.

Ronan cast his gaze around St. Dunstan warily. "This is why I never come to the actual City. It feels like death here."

"It feels like dark magic."

"Same thing. Anyone who plays with dark powers ends up steeped in darkness themselves. And darkness always leads to death."

I cast my gaze his way, lifting a brow. "Since when did you become so superstitious?"

"It's in my blood to be wary of magic I don't understand."

Shifters always had been, even if they carried magic in their own veins.

"Don't worry," I said, cracking a smile. "I doubt any ghosts will jump out and eat you. Probably."

Ronan strode over to me, leaning down to stare

deep into my eyes. My breath caught, despite myself. "If the ghosts are going to devour anyone, it's going to be you, love. Not me. You're the one who wants to poke around and find their stone."

"Speaking of…" I trailed off and glanced around, desperate for any excuse to change the subject…or, er, get away from Ronan's intense gaze. Even though we were in a creepy-as-hell bombed-out church, I didn't totally trust myself around him. My shifter side liked his attention, more than I wanted to admit. It was different than what Balor made me feel, but maybe that was a good thing.

Maybe that chest-tightening, heart-attack-inducing, all-consuming need was a bad thing. Especially now that I knew Balor had been responsible for the end of my family. Maybe I needed to forget about him. Maybe I needed to move on to something more normal.

Of course, nothing about Ronan was normal.

Ronan cocked his head, catching the strange, addled look on my face. "Everything alright, Clark? Don't tell me you've been possessed by a ghost."

I cleared my throat, glanced away. "I'm fine."

But he could tell I wasn't fine.

"What's going on?" The mocking look fell from his face as he placed heavy hands on my shoulders. "You've been acting odd ever since you came back from your Court. Did Balor say something to you?"

"Yes and no," I said around a mouthful of rocks. "I mean, he didn't say anything."

He frowned.

"Nemain said some things," I finally said. "About my family. About what Balor did to my family. Back

ONE FAE IN THE GRAVE

when my parents…did what they did, the Courts retaliated by killing every single member of my family. Turns out Balor was the one who made that order."

"I see." A beat passed. "To be honest, Clark, I'm not surprised. Balor has always had a taste for vengeance and violence. The fact that he let you and your grandmother live is much more shocking to me."

"I don't think he did. Let us live, I mean," I said quietly, unshed tears burning my eyes. "At least not on purpose. We escaped. He didn't let us go."

"Is that what he said?" he asked.

"Balor? No. But it's the only thing that makes sense," I said. "They were after us. Every single day, another member of my family was killed. If it wasn't for my grandmother, I wouldn't have survived."

"Nemain could be lying, you know."

"I wish she was. I really do." I sucked in a deep breath and blinked back the tears. "But she wasn't. I could tell."

Ronan fell silent, and then sighed. "I'm going to say something, but you probably aren't going to like it. Hell, I really should keep my mouth shut. The day my Pack died, I swore to myself that I would never get this involved in another person's life ever again. It's none of my damn business. Sticking your nose in where it doesn't belong is how you get your boots stuck in way too much shit."

"Are you going to say that my family deserved it?" I barked out a harsh laugh. "I think most of the fae agree. The only shame for them is that I wasn't taken along with the rest of them. I'm still alive. Much to their horror."

"I wasn't going to say a damn thing like that,

Clark," Ronan reached out, grabbed my arms, and shook them hard enough to snap me out of my stupor. "Stop talking so much shite. You know I don't want you dead."

I swallowed hard. "Then what is it that you wanted to say to me?"

"I was going to say that Balor Beimnech isn't who you think he is. Sure, he's good for London, for the supes as a whole. He struck up an alliance with the vamps, with the shifters, all for the hope of peace. That means he's better than most."

"I sense a 'but' coming along."

"A big 'but' I'm afraid." He sucked in a lungful of air. "You've put him up on this pedestal. You think he's some kind of hero. Right? The guy who is going to charge in on a beautiful horse and sweep you off your feet."

I snorted. "No. That would be ridiculous."

"It would be ridiculous, but that doesn't mean you don't want it." He slid his finger beneath my chin, and tipped up my head so that I had to look square in his eye. "Tell me you don't think of Balor and hope for it."

I swallowed hard. "I don't need anyone to save me."

But that didn't mean I didn't hope someone would try.

I could take care of myself, thank you very much. But that didn't mean I wanted Balor to stop trying.

"Of course you don't." He rubbed his thumb along my jawline. "And don't forget that, Clark.

Ronan stepped back, leaving a gulf of cold air in his wake. I stared after him as he began to wander the perimeter of the ruins, humming a classic Oasis song. He seemed totally unaffected by our conversation, by the bombshell he'd dropped on my head. He probably was. Balor, and the truth of his nature, had no effect on Ronan's life.

"I'll check this side of the ruins. You check over there," I finally said. I needed a moment alone with my thoughts. Ronan's words had rocked me. I thought I knew Balor. He'd let down his walls around me, or at least that was how it had seemed at the time. The cold, cruel face he showed to the world was all a lie.

But had it been? He must have done something to get that reputation, more than just pretend to sleep with girl after girl after girl. He sat on a throne of crimson skulls, bones taken directly from those he had conquered. Was my family a part of that throne? If my grandmother hadn't ferreted us away before his people had found me, would I be among those skulls as well?

Sucking a deep breath in through my nose, I pushed those thoughts aside. Regardless of whatever Balor had done—and what he'd meant to do—there were hundreds of fae in his House. Some were my friends. None of them deserved to die. I had to find the right Bullaun and reverse the damage before it was too late. After that…

I didn't know what I would do after that.

Picking through the ruins, I kept my eyes peeled for anything that looked like the photographs and drawings that Kyle had shown me. None of the cursing stones looked exactly the same, but they all had some similar characteristics. They all resembled an altar made of stone, covered in globular rocks of varying sizes. Some of the rocks sat clustered together, but the actual cursing stone—the Bullaun that held all the power—would sit in a curved indentation in the stone, a pool slightly larger than the rock.

But I didn't see anything like that here. All I found were crumbled pieces of the church, vines, and more vines. And then vines some more. In frustration, I started digging into the very depths of the vines, pushing my fingernails deep into the dirt in hopes I could unearth hidden treasures. The site had been bombed long after the stones had been created. Maybe they had been lost beneath the rubble. Maybe if I dug for long enough, I would find it.

Of course, that probably meant that Nemain hadn't found it either.

Which meant this wasn't the stone.

And, if that was the case, we had wasted way too much time already.

"Clark," Ronan's rumbling voice drifted toward me from where he stood on the edge of a pond. He waved me over, gesturing at the slight rippling water that jutted out beyond the edge of his thick boots. Deep beneath the surface, a carved piece of stone poked up from the ground. On top of it sat a single rock, sinking into a circular indentation.

I stared down at it, half-glad and half-annoyed. "So, that's the Bullaun."

"That's the Bullaun."

I pointed at it. "It's at the bottom of the pond."

"So it is."

"Do you think Nemain would have bothered to use that one? It seems like a bit of an inconvenience to fish a slab of rock out of a pond and then put it back down there."

Ronan was silent for a moment before he responded. "I don't think Nemain is too bothered about a slight inconvenience. She wants the Courts. If that means wading into a shallow pond, then she'll wade into the damn pond."

"You have a point."

Knowing what I knew about Nemain—which wasn't much, to be honest—I couldn't imagine some water stopping her from getting what she wanted. After everything she'd gone through to take Balor's Court, it was clear she was more than a little desperate to rule. Of course, Nemain also had plenty of lackeys willing and able to do whatever she commanded. Lesley had been evidence of that. She'd even killed in Nemain's name, taking down innocent fae solely to tarnish Balor's reputation.

"Right." I toed the water. It rippled against my touch, tiny tremors that morphed our reflections into ghoulish versions of ourselves. The image took me back to those days just after I'd followed my stepfather's orders to spy on the Princess. When I'd heard that she was dead, I'd wanted to curl up inside of myself and never look at a mirror again for fear of seeing the truth about what I'd done.

When I'd finally built up the courage to look at my reflection again, I hadn't seen Clark Cavanaugh. I'd seen a monster.

I wondered if that was what Balor saw now when he looked at me.

Fingers snapped in front of my face, pulling me back to the present. "Earth to Clark. Now ain't the time to daydream, love. There's something not right about this place. It gives me the willies."

"Sorry." I swallowed down my memories and turned toward Ronan. He didn't look at me like I was some kind of pariah, even though he knew everything. "This pond reminded me of…well, Nemain."

"Seems like a good sign. Now, get splashing around in there, tiny bird."

I toed off my boots and stuffed my socks inside of them before eying up the water. The thing with magic is, you never really know when it's going to bite. This water looked harmless enough, but there had to be a reason why the Bullaun was down there instead of up here. Over the years, it could have just sunk deeper into the Earth, or the truth could be a lot more ominous than that.

With a deep breath, I jumped off the mossy bank. Almost immediately, my feet hit the bottom of the pond. Soft muck slipped between my toes, and clouds of dirt shot up, swirling through the water and turning it to a shade that looked a lot like porridge. I braced myself, waiting for the inevitable magic to come charging at me. But nothing happened. No pain, no sparks, nothing.

Raising my eyebrows, I twisted to glance at Ronan over my shoulder. He was watching me carefully, arms crossed over his muscular chest. "Doesn't look like the Bullaun is going to kill me, so that's a plus."

"That's good, because I don't fancy jumping in there to save you."

What a gentleman.

With a deep breath, I plunged into the pool. The icy water swirled around me, stinging my skin. I gritted my teeth against the cold and peeled open my eyes. Everything around me was murky and hidden in shades of greys and browns. I threw out a hand, reaching for the Bullaun. My fingers wrapped around the rock, smooth to the touch.

I tried to remember Kyle's instructions as my lungs ached for air. I stared through the murk and twisted the stone to the left, muttering the words to myself in my mind. Would an unspoken spell even work?

After I'd finished the incantation, I waited. Seconds stretched out before me, my body desperate for a breath of smoggy London air. Nothing happened. The rock didn't move. It didn't glow. Magic didn't flow around me, its sweet ribbons of power curling around my body.

It didn't make sense. Even if this wasn't the rock, it should do something.

Which could only mean one thing.

This rock was dead. It wasn't the one Nemain had used for her spell.

11

I sputtered for air when I pushed up from the bottom of the pool. Water sprayed everywhere, droplets flying toward Ronan. He let out a grunt as I wiped my soaked hair out of my face. My lungs burned; my eyes ached. And I was pretty sure I smelled like a sewer.

Ronan reached out a hand and pulled me out of the pond. I fell against him, my feet tripping on a thick root. Ronan's strong arms wrapped around me, holding me upright. Our faces were only inches apart now, and his nose brushed against mine.

Heat filled my neck, an embarrassing, albeit welcome, relief from the iciness of the water.

Of course, I smelled like I'd been dipped into a vat of putrid stink. So, that was definitely sexy.

"Er, sorry." I cleared my throat and tried to find it within myself to step away from him.

His voice was gruff when he spoke. "Careful. You won't be able to help Balor if you break your neck."

Help Balor.

Just hearing my former Prince's name spoken aloud put a damper on the whole heated neck thing. "I'm not just helping *him*. I'm helping the entire Court."

I don't even know if I want to help him anymore…

Gently, Ronan extracted himself from my awkward arms. "And did it work? Has the curse been undone?"

I pressed my lips together and shook my head. "That would be a negative. I got nothing from the stone. It's like the magic isn't there anymore."

"A dead Bullaun. It's been used too many times. Probably why it ended up in the bottom of a pond."

I arched a brow. "You know more about Bullaun than you let on."

"I know a little," he said. "And I never said I didn't know anything about them. You didn't ask, and it seemed like you had a pretty good idea of what you were looking for."

"Well, it's dead. Now what?"

"Now, we get the hell out of this creepy-ass church."

With a heavy sigh, I turned back to take one last scan of the ruins. This had been a literal dead end, and time was quickly running out to save the Court. I knew when we'd come here that it had been a long shot, but the reality was hitting me hard. My mind flooded with conjured images of my friends' faces when I told them that I'd failed to find the right stone, that the countdown toward their impending deaths continued.

"It's alright." Ronan settled a warm, comforting hand on my shoulder and squeezed. "This isn't the end. There's still more, right? Just keep looking. You'll find the right stone."

I turned to face him, heart hammering. For once, his expression was earnest and free of the disinterest and disdain he usually carried around with him wherever he went. "Wow. These ruins really are doing a number on you. This is pretty much the only time you've ever said anything nice to me."

He scowled, dropped his hand away. "Don't get used to it, tiny bird."

"You're right. She shouldn't get used to it." A man stepped out from the shadows of the ruins. Well, a *man* might not accurately describe this dude. He towered over us, even Ronan, and he was about as wide as a tow truck. His muscles bulged against his tight black tank top, jeans ripped around the knees. They didn't look like much of a fashion statement though. The way his body pulsed made me think that he was about two and a half seconds away from shifting into a beast.

A low growl emanated from Ronan's throat, a sound that sent shivers along my arms. "Rock. What are you doing here? I thought I told you that I don't want to join your damn Pack."

My eyebrows shot even harder. "Pack? But I thought Anderson now ran the Pack."

"Different Pack, love," Rock replied. "We're distinct from the main pack. Mostly in that we want nothing to do with your vampire friends. Or the fae."

Well, that was certainly interesting and not in a

good way. If some of the shifters of London had begun to break away from the main Pack in direct opposition to Balor, then tensions between the supernaturals were going to be on even shakier grounds. Did Balor know?

"Leave her out of this," Ronan said in a harsh voice, edging just in front of me. I fought the urge to roll my eyes. I could take care of myself, thank you very much. "And like I told you, I'm not part of any Pack. I'm my own man, and I plan to stay that way."

"You're going to have to choose a side, Ronan. It's either us or it's them." Rock jerked his meaty thumb my way. "And she's one of them."

Ronan curled his hands into fists, his body practically humming with anger. "Are you threatening her?"

Oh boy. This was going to get bad fast unless I did something to stop—

Several more shifters slithered out from the shadows. One moment, the ruins had been quiet, still, and calm. And now it was teeming with wolves. Fairly impressive, I had to admit. Normally, the shifters were so clumsy and loud that you could hear them coming from five miles away.

"Listen, boys." I cleared my throat and moved out from behind Ronan's thick form. "Let's just all calm down."

"We'll calm down," the shifter said, punching his fist into his opposite palm, "when Ronan leaves all of this fae shite behind him and comes with us."

"Right," I said slowly, heart pounding in my chest when the handful of shifters began to stride toward us. It didn't look like we were getting out of this mess without a fight. "You know he's not a member of

Anderson's Pack, right? Isn't it enough that he wants to be independent?"

"Nope." Rock's eyes narrowed. "Not when he's helping a member of Balor's Court."

"Funny that. I'm not actually a member of Balor's Court anymore," I began. But it was no use. They'd already made up their minds. And so had Ronan. His body had begun to shift while I'd been spouting nonsense at the shifters. His muscles were rippling; his bones were crunching. Dark, wiry hair sprouted up along his arms, and his face transformed from the familiar, ruggedly-sexy face I knew and into something else.

Something…kind of scary, to be honest.

His nose expanded and lengthened, forming just above two rows of massively sharp teeth. His lips curled back, showing every single pointed end. A low growl exploded from deep within him, a sound so loud I was sure it would wake the dead. I reached for my sword and held it before me, wetting my lips as the shifters around us transformed into their beastly wolves.

I'd never fought a group of wolves like this before. I had no idea how my swordplay would work against them. Guess it was time to get a crash course.

The shifters rushed toward us. Ronan leapt forward. He crashed into Rock in the air, claws and jaws outstretched. A loud crack exploded into the night as their powerful bodies slammed together. Snarls filled the air. Fur and blood and flesh flew through the ruins.

Heart hammering hard in my chest, I watched in horror. It was impossible to tell what was happening.

Either Ronan was winning. Or he was dying. I couldn't bear to watch, but I also couldn't bring myself to pull my eyes away. Fear trembled through me. Not for myself but for the man who had welcomed me into his home and his life.

A snarl from behind me yanked my attention away from Ronan. Every hair on my neck stood on end as I slowly turned to face the shifter hunkered behind me. A low growl seeped from the wolf's open jaws. Saliva dripped onto the ground, forming a pool of disgusting slobber around its clawed feet.

I took a step back, tightened my grip on the hilt of my sword.

Another shifter stepped up beside him. And then another.

And then another.

I was surrounded by them. While I'd been distracted by the brawl between Ronan and Rock, the others had snuck up behind me. Four on one. It was smart. I'd give them that. While I was strong enough to take on one of these beasts with a sword—in theory—four at once put me at a great disadvantage. A pretty lethal disadvantage, if I were being honest. All it would take was one swipe of a single claw while I was fighting another, and that would be it. The wolves were massive. Twice as big as a normal wolf, not that I'd ever seen one.

I kind of needed some help.

And so did Ronan.

With a deep breath, I kept my gaze focused on the shifters before me but called out at the skies above. If I ever needed my raven friends, it was now.

The sky darkened above us. A boom shook

through the quiet night, rumbling the earth beneath our feet. Taking a deep breath, I held up my sword just as rain slashed down from the skies. Wind whistled through the ruins, a song full of danger and death.

The shifters looked excited. Their yellow eyes were lit up with anger and rage. They could no doubt sniff my fear, a tantalising scent drifting toward them on the wind.

And then a shifter leapt. He soared through the air, claws outstretched. Gritting my teeth, I held my ground and ignored the frantic beating of my heart. My palms were sweaty around the hilt of my sword; my stomach was in knots.

I ducked low just as the shifter reached me. He flew just over me, landing with a hard thud on the rocky ground. Sucking in a deep breath, I whirled toward him, knowing that I was leaving three more standing just behind me. Either way, I was surrounded.

His jaws opened wide as he stalked toward his prey. Every half-second, I shot a glance over my shoulder to see the other shifters standing by and watching. They wanted to see him attack me. They wanted to watch his claws rake through my body, my blood spill on the ground.

In the distance, I heard Ronan roar in pain. Tears sprang into my eyes, bitter and full of fire. We were going to lose this fight.

Where were my ravens? Why had they abandoned me this time?

The shifter stalked even closer.

I dropped back my head and screamed, "Help!"

That was when the sound of wings filled the

shadowy ruins. At first, it was soft, barely audible over the sound of rushing rain. But then it grew louder, and louder, and louder until the shifters began to turn their gazes up to the sky.

I shielded my eyes against the rain and stared up at the growing black cloud above us. It was a hundred flapping wings, dark feathers filling the rain-soaked sky. They cawed out screams, both of fear and of rage, seeing me surrounded on the ground.

Magic shot through me like fire. It curled in my gut, an animalistic response to the ravens in the air. They heard me. They saw me. They understood me, just as though we were joined together as one.

From behind me, I heard the crack of breaking bones and then, "What the hell?"

One of the shifters had transformed back into his human form, and he was standing there in the rain much like me. Hand over eyes, staring up at the gathering ravens.

"Those are my friends," I said to him with a smile. "If I were you, I'd get the hell out of here before they peck every last slice of skin from your face."

I'd seen the ravens attack on more than one occasion. It was bloody and brutal and terrible to behold. But I would not hesitate to turn them on these shifters if it meant saving both of our lives.

The shifter took one last glance at the sky, and then ran. The ravens swooped in low, screaming as they followed close behind him. Others landed on the shifters still in the ruins, their wings flapping wildly, their beaks sinking deep into flesh. Blood splattered everywhere, drenching the ruins in red.

Magic hurtled through me as the ravens continued

their attack. It was like an avalanche, twisting through me with a force I could barely stand. My head went fuzzy; my eyes went heavy. The last thing I saw before I fell to the ground was Ronan collapsing to his knees, eyes rolled back in his head.

He looked dead.

12

I cracked open my eyes. The stars were dim in the smoggy sky, but I could clearly see Jupiter's bright form bursting through the darkness. With a groan, I pushed up from the ground and glanced around me. Black feathers covered my body like a blanket. Dimly, I remembered the attack. There had been too many of them. The wolves had surrounded me.

With desperation pouring through my veins, I'd called out to the birds.

And I had become one myself.

A deep growl sounded from behind me. A growl that was more like a groan. Jumping to my feet, I spun to find Ronan's blood-soaked body sprawled beneath the shadows of the ruins. My heart jumped into my throat, and I rushed to his side, dropping to my knees to press shaking hands against his open wounds.

Blood was everywhere. It filled the air with iron. He was covered in cuts, gashes, and bruises. It was impossible to tell where his wounds ended and the blood began.

"Ronan," I whispered, tears falling from my eyes and plopping onto his skin. I'm so sorry I've gotten you involved in all of this."

This was my fault. If Ronan hadn't been helping me, this rogue Pack wouldn't have come after him, demanding he give in. They hated the fae. They hated me. And they'd taken his assistance as some kind of subservience to Balor.

"Don't you dare cry, tiny bird," Ronan said in a whisper I almost didn't hear. "I've survived. It's just a few scratches."

I choked out a bitter laugh. He was as stubborn as always, even when he was seconds away from death. With a deep breath, I dropped back my head and stared up at the sky, willing an answer to come to me. How could I save him? I wasn't a healer, and by the time I could get someone from the Court here, he'd already be gone. I knew it deep within my bones. These wounds would take him away from this world. It wouldn't take hours. It wouldn't take days.

It would take moments.

Precious moments that I couldn't slow or stop.

A warm finger reached up, grabbed the tear at the edge of my chin. "You don't need to cry for me, Clark. I can shift myself and heal."

A gasp popped from my throat. I glanced back down at him, heart battling against my ribcage. "You can heal?"

He ground his teeth together as he gave me a slight nod. "It'll hurt like hell, but I can do it. I'm going to need you though, tiny bird, if you think you're up for it."

"Of course I'm up for it," I said in a rush of words. "I'll do whatever it takes if it means you'll live."

"Good." He sucked a sharp breath in through his nose and closed his eyes. "Because it ain't going to be pretty either."

"Just tell me what it is you need me to do."

"Stay here by my side. Talk me through it. That's it. Just don't let me stop, even if I beg for it all to end."

My heart thumped hard. That sounded far more ominous than I'd expected.

I took his hand in mine and squeezed. "I'm here. I won't leave your side. Now, shift, Ronan. Shift before all your strength leaves your body."

That got him to start.

He cried out as ripples of pain shot through his body. Dark hair sprouted along his skin as his limbs ripped wildly by his sides. His arms grew longer and wider, and a deep-throated growl rumbled from his open mouth. Shivers stormed across him. I stumbled back, hand pressed tightly to my heart. I'd seen Ronan shift many times by now. He'd used his own highly-trained powers to show me how to get better with mine.

It had never looked this painful. It had always looked so easy.

Like changing from one jacket to the next.

It was hard to watch him go through this. It looked liked the worst pain anyone could ever experience. It was almost as though he had to die, over and over again, in order to live. I paced back and forth as he went through another shift, back into human form from the beastly wolf. He was left panting on the dirt-covered stones, his body curled into itself. He shivered, teeth chattering. Quickly, I dropped to his side and pressed my hand against his back. His skin was on fire, pulsing with an intense heat that almost burned my hand.

Swallowing hard, I stretched out beside him and wrapped my arm around his body, pulling him close. I had no idea what I was doing—or why—but it felt like the right thing to do in order to get him through this. He was hot, but he needed warmth. There wasn't much I could do to help him heal, but holding him close…that I could do.

Moments stretched out into hours. Ronan shifted into his wolf and back again. Over and over until his two forms seemed to blend together in my mind. When he was in his human form, I held him close. When he was in his wolf form, I kept my fingers wrapped tightly around his fur. He never spoke a word, but every now and then, he stared at me with eyes full of pain.

At some point, my own eyes fell shut, and I left behind the world for dreams.

Deep golden streaks shot across the night sky. Remnants of the sun that had been blazing high only hours ago. A wintry breeze whipped across the rolling hills, bringing with it the unmistakable stench of blood. Iron, death, and rot.

I stood on the hillside with a crimson cloak rippling around my legs. The warrior stood beside me, outfitted in a grey iron suit that protected his body from harm. Not that he would need it, not now. I would stride into battle beside him. And we would win.

He glanced my way, his eyes only visible through the thick helmet. "And you are certain we will win, my Queen?"

"Oh, yes. We shall win." My voice was full of power, a ghostly, phantom-like growl that drifted away with the wind. Down in the valley below us, our warriors—both male and female who had volunteered to fight for the crown—stood ready and waiting, swords and bows drawn.

Even without my power, the opposing army would find it difficult to win against my warriors. They had been trained and trained, night and day, until their hands bled and their feet crumbled underneath them.

Some had cursed me for the pain and suffering I had caused them. I did not blame them, nor did I punish them. They would soon understand the intensity of the training. They would fight, and they would win.

"My Queen." A female warrior strode up the bank of the hill. Her long, dark hair had been pulled back from her face, highlighting a strong jaw and yellow eyes.

"Nemain." I gave her a nod. "You should be at your station. Is there a problem?"

I had been watching Nemain closely these past months. There was a ferocity in her eyes that warned me there was more going on in her head than she let on. Her training had suffered because of it. She often gave up too easily, too early. Physicality was not her strong suit. She preferred to think.

"I heard a rumour that the Ivory Court plans to attack from the east instead of from the west." Nemain gestured behind us, at the empty green hills that stretched out as far as the eye could see.

I gave a sniff. "Impossible. My scouts are never wrong."

"Perhaps they are turning against you, against the Crimson Court."

I narrowed my eyes at the young warrior. What was she trying to accomplish here? Did she truly believe my scouts had lied to me, or had been wrong? A deep sense of dread settled in my gut. The Crimson Court could not be defeated. Not with me by their side. But that would not stop us from losing far too many fae. I did not want to see this battleground littered with bodies.

"I can go check it out myself," Nemain suggested. "I might not be a good fighter, but I can run fast."

I lifted a brow, glancing once at my second. "Are you trying to get out of the battle, Nemain?"

"Of course not," she said briskly. A shiver raced across her body, as if she were trying—and failing—to shake off the irritation she felt for her Queen. "I heard a rumour. I thought you should know."

Narrowing my eyes, I tried to sort through what this meant. Either Nemain was trying to get out of battle by being sent on a meaningless mission, or we truly did have our enemies coming for us from the wrong direction.

I turned to my second. "Are you fine here for now? The Ivory Court should not be here for another few hours."

"I will stand ground until you return, my Queen. Just be swift," he said.

Swift I could be. Because while Nemain might be fast on her feet, I was faster in the skies. With a deep breath, I transformed into my raven and soared through the skies. My conspiracy quickly joined me. No matter where I went, they were always there, waiting for my command or my unspoken need.

When I needed warmth, they were there. When I needed protection, they came to my aide. The bond I had with them was unlike any other, except for the one I had with my mate. The smiter.

We formed a unit as we flew to the east, me out in front, as always. Through my enhanced vision, I spotted the coast glistening in the distance. It made no sense for our enemies to come this way. They would have to find somewhere beneath those jagged cliffs to anchor an entire fleet. The winds being what they were, they would not find that easy.

Suddenly, an arrow whistled past my head. It hit one of my ravens. Blood arced through the air, splattering my wings. And then another arrow came. This one was for me.

Pain exploded from deep within me. It consumed my body and my mind until nothing else existed but a hundred tiny needles digging deep into my skin. I was falling. The world went black in the corners. I opened my mouth to scream, to call out my battle cry, to do anything to save those who were depending on me.

But when I opened my mouth, the only thing that came out was blood.

~

A hand touched my face, and I choked in big gulps of air. I sat up straight, grasping for blood-drenched wings. Instead, all I found was skin. I was okay. It had just been a dream. Nemain hadn't cornered me on the battlefield and tricked me into scouting in the east.

She hadn't lured me into a trap.

I was still alive.

"Whoa," Ronan said with a deep chuckle. "Careful. I'm still feeling a little sore after all that."

I swallowed down my gulps and pried open my

eyes as Ronan's hands wrapped around my elbows, holding me in place. He was naked before me, his skin clean and free of blood. More importantly, not a single cut was anywhere on him. He'd healed.

I let out a long exhale in relief.

"Oh my god. It worked."

He gave a nod. "It worked."

I reached out and touched the smooth shoulder. "How do you feel?"

"Like death." But he cracked a grin. "It was pretty damn painful, but a little sleep and a few beers, and I'll be good as new."

"I thought you were going to die," I said before I could stop the words from spilling out of my mouth. Another tear popped up in my eye, even though he was clearly fine now. There was no reason to cry, but I felt on the verge of tears all the same. "I was scared you weren't going to make it."

"Of course I made it." His smile slipped from his face as his eyes went dark. "I made it because of you, Clark. The way you sat there beside me, through it all. The warmth of you, your body…"

My skin went hot, and this time, it wasn't from the fever that had wracked him as he'd fought against his wounds. A need curled within me, a need I could see reflected in his dark eyes.

"I just did what you asked me to do," I said in a small voice.

He shifted closer to me, cupping my chin in his palm. Suddenly, I was extremely aware of his nakedness, even though he'd been like that for the endless hours I'd spent coaxing him through the healing shifts. Every single part of him was on display, including some very…*awake* parts. And it was awakening something in me, too, something I'd been doing my damnedest to push down.

"I want to thank you properly, Clark," he said in a low growl as his hands drifted down to my waist. "But you're wearing far too many clothes for me to do that."

My body trembled as he pulled at the edges of my black shirt. Despite all the warring thoughts in my head, I arched my back, letting him pull the soft material away from my skin. He let out an appreciative growl as his gaze drank me in, lust sparking in his eyes.

I sucked in a sharp breath as he dipped his head to mine. His lips drifted across my neck, softly and gently, before his teeth nicked my skin. Pleasure curled around my core. His hands slipped up my body, and then reached my breasts. I shuddered against his touch, pressing against him as my nipples hardened. I couldn't help but want him. The shifter part of me was crying out for his touch, begging me to give myself to him.

His mouth dropped to my breasts, and his tongue teased at my nipple. I arched my back and groaned, body writhing with need. Shockwaves of pleasure shook through me as his tongue and lips teased at my breasts, his hands now dropping to my waist again.

He pulled off my jeans in one quick motion, and then spread my thighs as he angled his body over mine. My legs hooked around his back, pulling him closer toward me. He paused for a moment, staring down at me with those lust-filled, dark eyes. My heart hammered hard in my chest, racing so fast that I could barely breathe.

My god, I wanted him. Even though I shouldn't, I did.

But then an image of Balor's face popped into my head, unbidden. His fiery eye, softened with affection. His slight, smirking smile that had so many times made my heart race. Guilt flooded through my gut. And I hated him in that moment. Here I was, with a man who wanted me. I wasn't doing anything wrong. I shouldn't have any loyalty toward Balor. He'd shut me out. Hell, he'd gone so far as prohibiting me from even being within ten meters of his property. I shouldn't feel this way. I shouldn't let him stop me from moving on.

But he was all I could think about.

Ronan frowned and pulled back. "There it is again. The look on your face when you're thinking of him."

"I'm sorry," I whispered. "I can't help it. No matter what I do, he's always there."

I expected Ronan to shout and yell. I expected him to make a big fuss of my response. He'd get angry. He'd explode into a rage that would bring the wolf right out of him. But what he did was even worse than that. He just sighed, pushed himself up from the ground, and walked away.

13

We didn't really have much to say to each other on the trek back to his warehouse. I kept trying to come up with an excuse, an explanation. But I didn't have one. Or, well, I *did* have an excuse, but the truth wouldn't make things any easier for either of us.

I was in love with Balor Beimnech.

Even though I shouldn't be. Even though I probably couldn't ever trust him again after this.

Not that he'd give me the chance.

"Speak of the devil," Ronan muttered as we strode up to his warehouse and found Balor himself waiting outside of it.

He was standing there with the light wind ruffling his hair, arms crossed over his chest. He looked like a Greek God statue, all hard planes and perfectly-sculpted features. It made me hate him even more, especially when my heartbeat picked up speed just at the sight of him.

Balor flicked his eye between me and Ronan. He

must have sensed something—or smelled it—because a slight flicker of pain went through his expression. Or maybe I merely imagined it, hoping he'd respond with jealousy when he would do nothing of the sort.

"You can't just show up here like this, mate," Ronan began without waiting for any sort of friendly greeting. He strode up to my former Prince, shoulders back. "You banished her. If she's not welcome on your property, then you're not welcome here."

Balor didn't react to Ronan's words. Instead, he turned to me. "One of my fae has fallen gravely ill. I need you to tell me everything you found out from Aed."

Ronan let out a grunt. "You finally believe her then. Well done on waiting until it was too late."

Balor cut his eyes toward Ronan. "You would do well to keep your mouth shut. I have no allegiance with you. I will not hesitate to put you in your place."

Ronan growled.

"Enough." I threw up my hands and stepped between them. "What are you talking about, Balor? Who fell ill? And how? What's wrong with them?"

Balor's jaw rippled as he clenched his jaw. "Cormac."

"Cormac?" Shock flittered through me. Of all the fae to fall ill, Cormac would not have been the one I would have guessed. He was one of the strongest of them, one of the longest living. He was like an immoveable rock. He wasn't much fun to be around most of the time, but there was no denying that he was damn good at what he did: kicking ass and taking names.

Balor gave a solemn nod. "Tonight…" He glanced

up at the brightening sky. "Last night, actually. He complained of a headache. I found that odd, but didn't think much of it. A few hours later, he was flat out on his bed, and couldn't move."

"Damn," I said slowly.

"Damn indeed."

I glanced up at him, and my heart squeezed tight. His face looked just as it had when I'd imagined him earlier. Handsome and sharp, full of strength. My heart skipped a beat, everything within me wanting nothing more than to reach out and pull him close, for us to erase the distance he'd put between us. He was here now. Had he changed his mind? And could I forgive him, if he had?

"I think I'll leave you two alone to talk," Ronan muttered, and then ambled on over to his warehouse door.

I turned to call out after him, but Balor grabbed my arm. He shook his head. "Let him go. This doesn't concern him."

Irritation flickered within me, chasing away my desire. "And this concerns me? I'm surprised you'd say that, considering that you chased me away from your Court…what, hours ago?"

His eyes flickered. "I explained to you why I had to do that."

"Because you don't trust me."

"Because I had to, Clark," he said in a low voice. "My people expect me to make difficult decisions in order to keep them safe."

My voice was a harsh whisper when I spoke, burning tears building in my eyes. "A few weeks ago, *I* was your people."

I had been more than just his people, but I couldn't bring myself to approach that particular side of our relationship. But there was no denying that we'd been a team. I had been his confidante, and he'd been mine. I had trusted him more than I'd trusted anyone else in my life, and I would have done anything in the world to stand beside him and his Court.

"The Court has always banished those they must," Balor said quietly. "It is the way of our world. It is as imbued in our lives as the bonds between a Prince and his subjects."

"Yeah, well," I said. "Maybe there's something wrong with the ways of your world."

"We don't have time for this," he said harshly. "Cormac is dying. Can we not put aside our differences if it means saving his life?"

"That's up to you, Balor."

He stared down at me. For a moment, I thought he'd turn away and storm right on out of there, leaving me to stew in my thoughts. But instead, he let out a heavy sigh. "I am sorry I didn't listen to you before. I need to know everything that's happened. Everything you know. It could mean saving Cormac's life."

"It could mean saving the lives of everyone, including yours." I explained to Balor everything I knew, and told him about my run-in with Nemain outside of his Court. He looked alarmed, but he let me finish the story before cutting in.

"So, Ronan and I found a Bullaun in London," I said as I rounded up the story. I decided not to mention the part about me sneaking into his Court and enlisting Kyle's help. "Unfortunately, that one was a dead end, so we'll have to go check out the others."

Balor slowly nodded, his eyes drifting off to stare at the horizon. "It has been a long time since anyone has used the Bullaun stones. There are always dark prices to pay. I thought the fae had finally let them go. I should have never assumed anything of the sort."

"Dark prices?"

His eyes cut to me. "Oh yes. The stone will never follow through with a curse unless something of great value has been sacrificed. Hundreds of years ago, fae were willing to pay that kind of price. Over the years, we learned better, and the use of the stones fell into nothing more than distant, dark memories. If anyone were to bring them back, I suppose I should have known it would be Nemain. She'll stop at nothing."

"I don't understand. Why does she want so badly to rule?"

"Power corrupts. It always has, and it always will. Either those who have it, or those who want it. She both has it and wants it, so she's more dangerous than most."

I took a step closer to him. "And what about you?"

He was quiet for a moment before answering. "Power must be checked, or it can become dangerous. I know that better than most."

"Because of what you did. Back when my parents killed your sister."

I hadn't really meant to bring this up now. It was a conversation for another time, but I'd been unable to stop the words from leaving my mouth.

Balor stiffened, and his expression went dark. "Nemain told you quite a bit then."

"So, it's true. She wasn't lying?"

"I gave the order."

I stared up at him, hardly believing the casual way he'd spoken those words. "So, you actually sentenced my entire family to die? Without a trial? The ones who were innocent? Including…including me?"

He ground his teeth together, refusing to meet my eyes. "It is more complicated than what you're saying."

"Well, then explain it to me!" My fists shook by my sides as my voice rang loud against the steel-encased buildings.

"What are you expecting, Clark?" His voice turned harsh as he strode from one end of the clearing to the next. "Some sort of explanation that can absolve me of what I did? You aren't going to get one. I made the order for your parents to die. Yes, without a trial. I didn't want them to have a chance to live. I didn't want them to get away with what they did. I wanted revenge. And I got it."

I stared at him, mouth open wide. "And so you wanted me to die, too. For what? To punish them? Don't you think their own deaths was punishment enough?"

"No," he said quietly as he stopped to stand before me.

"No, what?" I demanded.

He let out a heavy sigh, closed his eyes. "My fae… after they killed your parents, their bloodlust could not be sated. They weren't satisfied. So, they went after the rest of your family. They went after you. I…I thought they had killed you, too."

Tears burned in my eyes. "What are you saying?"

"I am saying that I am responsible for what happened to your family. But no, I did not order my fae to kill them or kill you. And those who committed such horrible atrocities in my name have paid for their crimes."

Relief shuddered through me. I hadn't wanted to believe that Balor was capable of what Nemain had said, but I'd also known what grief could make a person do.

He hadn't made the order. Not for innocents to die. That wasn't Balor.

I placed my palm on his chest, swallowing hard. Heat pressed back against me, and his magic curled around my fingers like a familiar caress. "I knew you didn't do it."

He tensed, pulled my hand away from his chest, and stepped away. "Just because I came to you for help with Cormac does not mean that things have changed between us."

"Of course not," I said bitterly. "Why trust the girl who would do anything to save your Court?"

His expression darkened. "I am sure you wouldn't do *anything*, Clark. Would you truly leave Ronan if that meant returning to your place beside me? I imagine not. I can smell what happened between the two of you."

My heart thumped hard, heat filling my cheeks. "Your power isn't perfect, Balor. You can smell things, but that doesn't mean you know the truth. But I don't have to explain myself to you."

"No." His red eye flickered, and then he turned away. "You don't."

Balor began walking away from the warehouse, his

hands hanging heavily by his sides. I frowned after him, my heart desperately wanting him to turn around and come back. "Where the hell are you going? What about Cormac? We have to go find the next cursing stone."

He froze, cast a glance over his shoulder. "*I* have to go find the next cursing stone. This has nothing to do with you."

"The hell it doesn't." Narrowing my eyes, I stormed toward him. "Look, I know you don't want me near you or your fae, but you can't pretend like this isn't important to me. And you can't act like my powers wouldn't help you find a way to reverse this damn curse. Moira, Elise, Kyle. They're my friends. Hell, they're my family. I would do anything to save them. Don't refuse to let me help."

He kept his back turned toward me, but his shoulders slumped, just a bit. "Fine. You can join Moira and Duncan on their quest to find the next stone. But don't bring too much attention to yourself. I don't want to have to explain to the other Houses why I'm letting my sister's murderer roam free."

And with that, he was gone.

14

*R*onan looked like a cat in a dog pound. He stood in the middle of the Court's command station, his skin practically jumping off his body. "Why did I agree to come along on this insane mission again?"

It was a good question. When I'd told him what I planned on doing, I hadn't even had to ask him to join me before he was volunteering himself, like some kind of knight on a white horse.

I couldn't help but wonder if he was taking his own words about Balor and his knighthood seriously and trying to prove that he was the one I could count on. And, to be honest, I could see that he was. I wasn't blind. I wasn't an idiot. Logically, Ronan ticked all the right boxes.

But the heart didn't always play by logic.

Speaking of…

"Where's Balor?" I asked, glancing around. He wasn't one to be late. In fact, it was one of his many pet peeves.

"He's not coming." Moira shot me an apologetic look. "He's dealing with some shifter business while we go hunt down this stone."

I exchanged a glance with Ronan. The shifter business no doubt had something to do with the rogues who had broken off from the main Pack. I'd meant to bring it up to Balor before, but I'd been so distracted by our infuriating conversation that I'd forgotten to fill him in on what we'd encountered in the church ruins.

"So," Moira continued. "It's just you, Ronan, me, and Duncan."

"That's an odd team," I said.

She shrugged. "Duncan insisted on coming. He's freaked out about Cormac. Thinks we can't manage this ourselves."

He and Cormac had always been inseparable. They were like two halves of the same coin, always a constant, always a team. I couldn't say I blamed him for feeling the need to get his hands stuck in so he could do something himself. He would probably go crazy if he tried to wait it out here. For once, I understood Duncan.

"We're going to take a car, and then ferry on over there." Moira spread a map out on the table before us, pointing to our route. It wasn't exactly the quickest way to get to Ireland.

"Shouldn't we take a flight?"

She gave a quick shake of her head. "The Fianna have been monitoring all flights from London to Ireland. Going by car and boat is the only way to get there without being detected."

"It'll take an entire day. And we just don't have

that kind of time to waste."

"Nemain can't know what we're up to," she said. "Balor's orders."

Moira was right. Of course she was. I just hated that we had to spend our precious hours avoiding detection from the very fae who had wreaked the havoc we were trying to reverse.

"Don't worry." Ronan shot me a wolfish smile. "I'm a fast driver."

∼

*R*onan hadn't been lying. Speed limits were merely pesky suggestions he thought best to ignore as the tiny car flew around the many bends and curves of the country roads. Moira had chosen a route that took us far outside the motorway's many cameras, instead directing us down skinny road after skinny road until I was certain my breakfast would end up on the windscreen.

I gritted my teeth as we whipped around another curve, tree branches scraping the sides of the tiny electric car. "Is this really necessary?"

He twisted to face me, only one hand on the wheel. "You said you wanted to get there fast. So, I'm getting you there fast."

A new wave of nausea bubbled up in my throat as the road dipped suddenly downward. I placed my forehead against the cool glass of the window, vision blurring. Moira placed a comforting hand on my shoulder. "Want me to hold your hair back while you chunder everywhere?"

"I'm not going to chunder everywhere."

"You're totally going to chunder everywhere."

Moira ended up being right, but it wasn't Ronan's bonkers driving that got me. After the whole driving whiplash, we boarded a ferry to cross the Irish Sea, and the churning waves were enough to send me heaving over a railing.

"I take it you've never been on a boat before," Moira said, holding back my hair as promised. "It doesn't suit everyone."

I sucked in a deep breath of cooling sea air and pushed away from the railing. "You don't seem fazed by it. Or Ronan's driving."

She shot me a grin. "I've got a steel stomach. Nothing fazes me, not even undercooked meat."

I wrinkled my nose, and Moira's smile dimmed. She turned suddenly, casting her eyes across the boat. The ferry was packed full of tourists, but that wasn't anything to be alarmed about. Frowning, I tried to steady myself and see what had caught Moira's attention.

"I swore I heard something," she muttered underneath her breath.

I stepped up beside her, shielding my eyes from the sun. "Heard what?"

She shook her head, her high ponytail of golden hair bouncing around her shoulders. "I must be tired."

"What do you think you heard, Moira?" I asked.

She pressed her lips tightly together. "I could have sworn I heard someone say Nemain. And something about her being in the waters ahead of us."

Chills swept along my skin, and I turned to gaze out at the churning waters. The sun was bright and beaming down on the sea, but everything was still cast in shades of grey. In the distance, I could see the lands of the Irish. No other boats. Nothing to indicate that our biggest enemy was out there waiting for us to pass.

"If she's out there, do you think she's waiting to ambush us?" I couldn't help but ask.

"What else would she be doing?" Moira asked quietly. "She's not out there for shits and giggles. I just don't know how she could have found us. We did our best to take a route unseen."

"Maybe this means we're headed to the right Bullaun. If she thought we might come here to try and reverse the curse, then she might have staked out some points along the way, just to make sure we didn't find it."

"Well, I don't know what we're going to do." Moira turned once again to face the tourists. "There's at least a hundred innocent humans on board. If she tries to sink this ship in order to stop us, they might all end up dead."

A new wave of chills rolled down my back. She was right. If Nemain tried to take down this ship, we weren't the only ones who would pay the mortal price. All these humans would die. Nemain wouldn't do a damn thing to try and save them. She'd made it more than clear where her priorities were. She would sacrifice a thousand innocents if it meant she could get her thrones.

"Right." I threw one last glance over my shoulder at the waves before turning toward the stairs that led below deck. "We can't let her do this."

Moira followed quickly behind. "What are you going to do, Clark? You aren't going to try to swim out and stop her, are you? The waters are crazy here."

"No. I'm going to fly."

I took off down the stairs and headed toward the toilets. With all the humans here, I couldn't very well shift into a raven on deck and leave shreds of clothing behind. For once, I would have to approach this whole thing with a little strategy. I just had to hope I had enough command over my bird form for it to work. In the past, I'd always had to rely on extreme emotions to get me to that point.

I was feeling a hell of a lot of emotions though. Anger, fear, and a shedload of frustration. I was sick and tired of Nemain, of her plots and her ploys. She'd been with me pretty much every step of the way my entire life. I couldn't shake her no matter where I went or who I became. She needed to be stopped, once and for all. And she needed to answer for what she'd done.

Moira followed me into the women's toilets, tapping her hand against the hilt of her hidden sword. "Are you sure this is a good idea?"

I cast a glance over my shoulder at her. "Nope."

"What will you do when you see her? Dive bomb her?"

"I haven't figured that part out yet." I pulled off my shirt and dropped it onto the floor. "First, I'm just going to scout ahead, see if I can spot anything. I won't go after her unless I have a good shot."

Moira nibbled on her bottom lip. "Clark…I don't like the idea of you taking her on like this. Alone."

"She's ruined my life, okay?" I stepped up to my friend, took her hands in mine, and squeezed tight. "She needs to be stopped and for more reasons than one. Not only because of what she did to me and my family but for what she'll do to so many more. She's never going to stop. You understand that, right? Even if we manage to undo this curse, she'll just keep coming at us. Over and over again until she takes everything she can. Maybe I won't be able to stop her either, but I have to try."

"I wish I could come with you."

"No, I need you to stay here. If I don't come back, I need you to tell Balor…"

Tears welled in Moira's eyes. "Tell him what, Clark?"

My heart thumped hard in my chest, and I glanced away. "You know what I want you to tell him."

"I do," she said quietly. "But you need to say it out loud. For yourself, more than anything. If you're going to go rushing off into danger like this, you need to say it."

"I can't." Pain lanced through me at the thought of admitting it out loud.

Moira's grip on my hands tightened. "Say it."

I swallowed hard and wet my lips. "I love him. Tell him I love him."

"Good." She let go and stepped back. "Now, hurry up and do this so you can get back. Because you're going to tell him yourself."

I barked out a laugh. Like I would ever manage that. Not only could I barely begin to admit my feelings to myself, I couldn't go and tell a male who hated me that I loved him.

But never mind that. I had an arsehole Princess to track down before hundreds more innocents met their untimely deaths.

With a deep breath, I toed off my jeans and

opened the porthole. I focused on my churning emotions, on the anger and the fear. Feathers sprouted along my arms, and my eyesight sharpened. Soon, I was out the window and soaring above the sea. My wings flapped underneath me. Wind poured into my lengthened face.

The bird inside of me screamed to push out, to take control of the tumbling skies. But I had to focus. I had to keep a tight hold on Clark. If I let the animal inside of me fill my mind, then I would never do what had to be done.

I soared over the seas, setting my enhanced sight on the waters that led to the Irish shore. Where would Nemain be, if she were waiting to ambush us? On some kind of boat? It seemed unlikely. These weren't the days of old where battles were waged in ships with cannonballs.

Did they even make those kinds of ships these days?

Probably not.

So, she'd have to have some other plan up her sleeve. One thing I'd learned about Nemain, she tried to avoid full-on battle whenever possible. Memories of my dream suddenly filled my head, of a Nemain tricking the Morrigan into leaving her army on the battlefield.

But that had just been a dream. Nothing more. My subconscious coming up with a bizarre story based on all the craziness going on in my life. It wasn't reality, and a firm grip on the facts was what we needed right now.

Still, I couldn't help but find the timing of the dream kind of…unsettling, to say the least. There were some parallels with my life that I definitely couldn't ignore. Nemain setting a trap, one that involved scouting ahead. Had she purposefully tried to lure me away from the ferry?

With a deep breath, I spun in a circle and headed straight back the way I'd come. A strange unease had settled over me, one that put a shot of fear into my heart.

It felt like someone was watching me. Like a pair of eyes were noting my every move. Even as I flew toward the ferry instead of continuing the scout across the waters, that feeling followed me with every beat of my wings.

Maybe it *had* been a trap. Maybe Nemain had planned to knock me from the sky. I hadn't seen a boat, nor had I seen any indication that she was sitting there waiting for us to arrive.

But that didn't mean she wasn't there, somehow.

We were going to have to be more careful. Even though my dream had been just that—a dream—it felt like a warning as well.

Nemain would do whatever it took to win.

But I would do everything in my power to stop her.

15

"Do you still feel like we're being watched?" Moira whispered to me as Duncan checked us into the pub's hotel.

"Yep." After I'd soared over the seas, I'd headed straight back to the ship where Moira had been waiting for me. As soon as she'd closed the porthole, I'd lost consciousness, the bird finally taking over my mind. She'd left me in there to…I don't know, flap around for awhile or something. When I'd finally come to, I'd gone straight to her and explained the feeling I'd encountered. I'd half-expected her to laugh me away, but she'd taken me seriously.

I still couldn't explain it. It almost felt like a dream. But I couldn't shake the sensation of the magic. The watchful eyes. The caress of hands along my feathers.

Someone was keeping an eye on us. Whether it was Nemain or something else…

"We're all checked in," Duncan said, joining us by the marked wooden table in the corner of the beer-laden pub. He held up a set of keys, jingled them.

"Just in case we need it, this'll be our base. Anyone gets lost? Come straight here. Hopefully we won't need it."

I arched a brow when he dropped a key in front of each of us, all attached to a fob that read number five. "Don't tell me the Court can't afford for each of us to have a room." I cut a glance at Ronan. The idea of sharing a bed with him after what had happened between us…

Duncan snorted. "Calm your tits. It's not like we're on holiday. We're literally not even going to sleep here. It's just a base of operation in case something comes up."

"It's possible we might have to stay a night," I pointed out. "If things take longer than we plan, which they often do."

"Then, we'll deal," he said slowly, crossing his arms over his chest. "One room and one room only. It's the best way for us to keep track of everyone."

It was almost like he didn't trust me to be let loose on my own. Or maybe Balor had told me that he had to keep an eye on me. I wrinkled my nose at the thought.

"You know I'm not your enemy, Duncan," I said. "I can see why it might seem that way to you, but I'm really not. All I care about is the Court. It's honestly all that matters to me. That's why I'm here."

Duncan was quiet for a moment, grinding his jaw together, eyes cast firmly on the marked wooden surface of the table. "I know. I wouldn't have agreed to come here with you if I didn't know how much you care about them all. I actually like you, Clark. Just don't tell anyone else that, okay? I have a reputation to uphold."

"A reputation of grumpiness," Moira added with a slight smile.

Duncan scowled.

"Now," he said, motioning over the waiter that was flitting around the room. "Let's have a bite to eat, and then let's find this stone. Don't order anything complicated. We need to get back on the road."

∽

The hills were wet and green, thick tree trunks rising high into the grey-streaked sky. We'd driven about two hours outside of Dublin to find the reported location of the second cursing stone. It was hidden deep within the wilderness, a long hike from the nearest car park. We crunched through twigs and piles of leaves, ambled across hills, and dipped deeper into a forest.

And that same strange feeling followed us every step we took.

"Those eyes are still on us," I said quietly after we'd been hiking for a solid three hours. My feet were beginning to ache, and my thighs burned every time we had to climb another hill. Unlike the others, I did not have limitless energy. I needed a break. Or a chocolate bar.

Maybe both.

Duncan cast me a skeptical look. "It is extremely unlikely that anyone followed us all the way from the pub to here, especially without being seen."

"Did you try casting your mind out again?" Moira asked me.

"Yep," I said with a frown. "I can't hear anything. All I can do is feel it."

"It's no wonder you're paranoid, after the way she popped up out of nowhere in London," Duncan said. "But look around us. She's not here, Clark."

I shot a glance at Ronan. He hadn't said much since we'd arrived in Dublin, but he'd never been much of a big talker anyway, so I hadn't thought much of it.

"Something is off," he finally said, boots crunching down stray twigs. "It feels a lot like it felt in those church ruins. Wrong."

My frown deepened. "You don't think the shifters followed us here, do you?"

"Why would the shifters have followed us?" Moira asked.

"Rogue shifters. They attacked us in the ruins. They're not big fans of Balor."

"Well, shit," Moira said. "That must be what Balor is dealing with back home. I hope he hasn't decided to go after them. He doesn't have backup while we're here."

A small seed of worry sprouted in my gut, but there was no reason for it. "Balor can take care of himself. With his eye, no one could ever take him down, at least not physically. Those shifters aren't exactly strategical masterminds. They just want to fight."

"Can confirm," Ronan said with a grunt. "They just want to see blood on the ground, and they're no match for Balor the smiter. None of us are, apparently."

Ouch. That was a serious dig in my direction. One that was, unfortunately, too close to the truth. But it did loosen the tight grip that worry had on my gut. Balor was a strong fighter. His weapon of choice was a sword. But he used his flaming eye when necessary. If those shifters went after him, they wouldn't stand a chance.

Still, something felt off. Something kept niggling me in the back of my mind. It had felt like someone was there, some unseen eyeballs following us wherever we went. But what if it wasn't that at all? What if it was something much more ominous than that?

I had no idea what. But I also had a feeling we would find out.

The path through the woods stopped abruptly. Before us sat three crumbling stone stairs that led to another wider stone platform higher than the tops of our heads. I gazed up at the structure, heart flickering inside of my chest. It was much larger than the sunken platform Ronan and I had found in the city, but there was no mistaking what it was. As we climbed the stairs, I could clearly spot three small stones sitting in sunken crevices dotted around the platform.

We'd found the second Bullaun.

We all stared down at it. No one said a word. All we could hear was the rustle of the wind through the leaves.

"So…" Duncan turned to me. "Do we just smash it?"

"Probably not a good idea," I said. "We need to

figure out if this is the right Bullaun first. Otherwise, we won't know if we have to go find the others."

Duncan crossed his arms over his chest. "And you know how to do that?"

I shot him a look of annoyance. "Yes. Don't act so surprised."

"I just didn't think you could do all that much other than read people's minds."

I decided to ignore him. Duncan was still salty with me, and that was fine. He didn't need to be my best friend in order for me to help the Court. It had been made more than clear to me that I only had a handful of friends in House Beimnech.

I knelt beside the stone and placed my palms flat against the smooth surface. Whoever had created this magical object had put a lot of time and energy into carving, sanding, and staining it to match. There was a darkness to the rocks that was unnatural, almost as though it had been dipped in old blood.

Closing my eyes, I forced my mind to focus on the object. In the old church ruins, it had been clear almost instantaneously that the magic had left the Bullaun behind. This was different. As soon as my fingers touched the surface, a hum of electricity answered my call.

A flicker of excitement ran through me. Slowly, I muttered the words Kyle had spoken to me. Words that I did not understand. They flew from my parted lips, dancing on the wind before vanishing into the distance.

This stone will destroy Balor Beimnech, once and for all.

My entire body stiffened. It was Nemain's voice, coming straight from the cursing stone.

I nodded and stood, excitement prickling the hairs on my arms. "That's it. That's the one. Not only has it been used recently, but I can hear Nemain's voice when I listen hard. She was here. She used these stones."

"Good. Now, reverse it."

I shot a quick glance at Ronan. "Well, here's the problem. No one really knows how to do that. Kyle had some suggestions for things to try. He thought that if we turned the stone in the opposite direction and sent the right energy into it, that might be what does it."

"That sounds like a bunch of mumbo jumbo to me," Duncan said quietly. "Cormac's life is on the line here. We can't fuck around."

"I think we should give Clark's thing a go," Moira said. "Kyle's a smart fae. He's done the research. He thinks this is what needs to be done."

Duncan arched a brow. "And has Kyle ever undone a Bullaun curse himself?"

"No."

"What if," he continued, "that by turning the stone some more, you release more of the curse onto the Court?"

"I don't think that's going to happen," I argued. "Kyle did the research. He told me what we need to do."

I stepped up to the stone again and twisted it in the opposite direction. Nothing happened.

Ronan frowned. "Something still feels off."

"Off how?" Duncan asked.

"I feel it, too," Moira added. "For what it's worth. There's something wrong in the air. It's hard to put my finger on what it is, but it's just there, hiding in the background."

"You've all gone mad," Duncan said with a grunt. "It probably feels wrong because we're standing here in front of a magical stone that can curse people. As soon as we get out of here, we'll feel better again. The only question is, did Clark reverse the curse?"

I pursed my lips, staring down at the Bullaun. I'd followed Kyle's directions and turned the stone in the opposite direction. In theory, that would have worked. But it didn't *feel* like it had worked. No magic had swirled through the air. The rock hadn't vibrated and shook.

It just sat there, as if I'd done nothing at all.

"I'm not sure," I finally said. "But I have a bad feeling about messing with it anymore. I know you don't feel it, Duncan, but something isn't right here. And I'm pretty damn certain it has something to do with that stone."

"So, how the hell are we going to destroy the curse then?"

I sucked in a deep breath and shook my head. "I don't know."

16

"Look, I'm just going by what Kyle said, okay?" I threw up my hands. "He told us exactly what we needed to do. And when it comes to magical stones that can curse people, I'm pretty sure it's a bad idea not to follow the prescribed procedure."

Duncan snorted. "Prescribed procedure. You make it sound like it's some kind of remedy from a doctor. Well, I'll have you know, Cavanaugh, that sometimes magic is a lot more complicated than that."

"You called me Cavanaugh." My voice went soft, which was a first when it came to Duncan. I knew we'd come to a bit of an understanding, but it was still a shock to see him using the name I'd chosen for myself, instead of the name everyone had deemed it necessary to call me.

He grunted. "'Course I did. I'd never call you a McCann. Well, not now, anyway. Maybe I did the first few days after the whole bombshell dropped at the Circle of Night."

"Thanks for that," I said. "And I mean it. No sarcasm."

He grunted again. "Don't get too sappy over it. I'm with Balor on your banishment. And I still think you're wrong about the stone. The whole reversing thing didn't work, did it?"

I pursed my lips. "No, I don't think it did. Something would have happened if the curse had been undone."

With a nod, he turned to Moira. "Any ideas?"

"My ideas all revolve around getting the hell away from this place as soon as possible." She frowned and glanced at the thick canopy of trees that surrounded us. "Maybe it's the wrong stone. If Kyle's instructions didn't work, then this is probably another dead end."

"But Clark heard Nemain's voice when she listened to the stone." Duncan turned toward me. "Didn't you?"

"Yes." I frowned. "But maybe she came here and didn't use it."

He shook his head. "We can't risk it. If this is the one, we have to take care of it. There's no other way to ensure that the House is safe."

"I really don't think we should destroy the stone, Duncan," I said.

"Are you in charge here?" he asked, crossing his arms over his chest. "Or are you merely along because Balor was sick of you poking around at Court?"

Ronan let out a low growl, but I motioned for him to stop. "Fine. It's up to you, Duncan. I just don't think it's a good idea."

"That's fine," he said, taking a swaggering step

forward while drawing his sword. "I'm more than happy to do the honour."

Duncan held up the hilt of his sword and slammed it down on the stone. I watched in horror as the pieces broke apart, as chunks of rock flew through the clearing. The sky overhead crackled, red streaks shooting through the clouds. It looked as though the sky was on fire, burning up from the force of the magic that had been destroyed. Heart hammering hard, I didn't dare breathe.

"There." Duncan grinned. "Curse broken. We can all go back home now. And you can go back to your hidey hole with your shifter friend here. We won't be needing your assistance anymore, Clark. But…" He sucked in a deep breath. "I do appreciate you doing everything you could for the Court. And I mean that. No sarcasm."

My lips twitched, and I gave a nod. "You sure you're feeling okay? You're acting far too much like you're fond of me. You might ruin your reputation, you know."

A wide grin spread across his face. I started to move toward him, out of a strange instinctual need to give him some sort of hug or pat on the back. But halfway to his side, his expression transformed completely. One moment, he wore the widest grin I'd ever seen on Duncan. The next, his face was twisted up in pain. His eyebrows were furrowed; his teeth jammed together.

He fell to the ground, his entire body twitching. No sound came from his throat. The pain was so great that he couldn't even breathe. His face went red, his hands clasping at his neck.

I fell to my knees by his side, placing my hands on his arms, on his neck, on his face. He was blazing hot, as if his body had been consumed by fire. Wordlessly, I shook my head, shock and horror pouring through me.

"I don't know what to do." I glanced over at Moira who had squatted on his other side. She looked just as horror-stricken as I felt. "What the hell is happening to him?"

Moira shook her head, her hands pressed tightly to Duncan's arms as if holding him in place would help. "I have no idea, Clark. I've never seen anything like this before. It's like he's having a seizure, but faeries don't have seizures."

Ronan strode from side to side with his hands jammed into his hair. "Shifters don't either. But humans do. Check his tongue. Make sure he isn't choking on it."

Gritting my teeth, I leaned over Duncan's shaking body and pressed a hand to his mouth. His tongue was nowhere near his throat. He wasn't choking, but the heat pouring through his mouth burned my hand.

I yanked it away, pressing my fingers against the wet grass. Instantly, they cooled, but the throbbing sent new shockwaves of pain up my arm.

"What the hell?" I frowned as I held my hand up before me. All of my fingers were bright red. "He burned me. Duncan's skin burned me."

Moira rocked back on her heels and stared down at our fellow warrior. The shaking had begun to slow, the redness in his face so bright that it made his eyeballs look like two large eggs. Slowly, the shaking faded into nothing but a twitch.

His body stilled. His face went slack. And then there was nothing left in his gaze, nothing but death.

Tears pouring down my face, I leaned over him once again and held my ear an inch away from his mouth. Not a single breath stirred against my hair. I sat back, pulled in a lungful of air, and dug my fingernails into the ground.

"He's dead," I said. "Duncan is gone."

17

A cackling laugh shot through the eerie silence. It was a laugh I'd heard in my dreams. One that had followed me all the way from my hidden home in America to where I'd landed here, in this forest, with Duncan's dead body lying at my feet.

Nemain stepped out from behind a wall of trees, several Fianna surrounding her. She clapped her hands, once, twice, thrice. And then the wicked smile fell from her face. "Well done. Aed told me he didn't think I'd be able to play you like a fiddle, but I'm glad he was wrong. Every time I want something done, I think to myself, 'Can I get Clark McCann to fall into my trap once again?'"

"Cavanaugh," I said through gritted teeth.

My veins boiled with anger as I stared at her smug face. Ronan growled, and Moira drew her sword. All of it was useless. Duncan was already dead, and we were far outnumbered. We could try to take Nemain out of the picture, and we might win the fight. But we'd never get to her. Not like this.

"What have you done?" I asked. "How did you set the stone up to kill Duncan?"

"I didn't set the stone up to do anything." She smiled again, this time wider and fuller than she had before. "That stone right there. It wasn't the cursing stone. It wasn't a Bullaun at all."

Confusion rippled through me. "But it was there on the platform. I held it in my hands. It was magic."

"Oh, it was magic alright, but not the kind you thought." Nemain took a step closer. Moira raised her sword, Ronan growled. For a moment, I saw a flicker of hesitation in Nemain's eyes, and I couldn't help but be satisfied that she still found us intimidating, even when surrounded by her loyal Fianna.

"We know it's not the same damn magic," Moira said in a low hiss. "Just tell us what you did. Or I swear to god I will swing this sword at your neck, and I don't care how many of your Fianna try to stop me."

Another flicker of hesitation, and then a laugh. "This one has a temper. No wonder you like her. Your mother was very similar. All one had to do was look in your direction, and she snapped."

It was my turn to growl, my eyes flashing as a new rage poured through me. Regardless of what my mother had done, she'd still been family. Besides, if anyone was to blame for what had happened, it was the manipulative arsehole Nemain had set upon my family like a scorpion with more venom than he knew what to do with.

Nemain's eyes flicked over to Ronan. "And I honestly don't know how *you* survived. The rogues I chose were some of the strongest shifters I've ever met. Says a lot about you and your survival skills. If you'd

ONE FAE IN THE GRAVE

rather join the winning team, I'd love to have you by my side. You're free to keep your cute little warehouse, of course. I'll let you remain independent. All you have to do is be my hired hand when you're needed."

I sucked in a sharp breath and glanced at Ronan. As an outsider, as an independent wolf, he had no allegiance to Balor's Court. He'd made that clear on more than one occasion. He wanted nothing to do with the fae and their political manoeuvrings, no more than he wanted anything to do with the London Pack.

"If I recall correctly," he said in a low, dangerous voice, "it was the Fianna who brutally murdered every single member of my Pack. Balor, on the other hand, never raised a hand to me or any of mine. And this fae right here," he said, jerking his thumb toward me, "is why your planned attack on me with the rogues didn't work. She's why I'm alive. So, I'll stay right where I am, thanks."

I turned back her way, my heart hammering hard at Ronan's words. Maybe he had more vested interest in our cause than I'd thought. He might not be Balor's biggest fan, but it was clear he respected him as a Prince. And, for the kind of man that Ronan was, that made all the difference in the world.

Also, Nemain kind of sucked.

Her smile dimmed, and it was quickly replaced with a scowl. "Wrong choice, wolf. Balor Beimnech's reign over the Crimson Court will soon come to an end. I can guarantee you that. Without his flaming eye, he is nothing more than a normal fae warrior. He is no longer indestructible. He is no longer unbeatable. His loyal subject, Duncan, has seen to that."

My heart thumped hard, and my world seemed to

narrow on Nemain's cruel face, the rest of existence dropping away until there was nothing else but her yellow eyes. "I don't understand."

Nemain lifted her chin and smiled. "The stone you destroyed was the sling stone."

I stared at her blankly. "The what now?"

"Fuck," Moira hissed, shifting slightly on her feet, as if she had to keep herself steady from the force of Nemain's words.

I shot her a quick glance out of the corner of my eye, not wanting to take my gaze fully off of Nemain and her Fianna. "What's she talking about, Moira?"

A tear slipped out of her eye and slid down her cheek. "The sling stone. We thought it was hidden. We thought no one could ever find it."

"But what is it?" I asked. Moira was clearly shaken. I'd never seen her even close to being on the brink of tears. She was like a solid rock. Unbendable, much less breakable. If Nemain's words were freaking her out, then we were in far more trouble than I'd thought.

"The magical world works in very interesting ways," Nemain began, lacing her hands behind her back. "It likes balance. Much like you guessed, if there is a way to cast a curse, there is also a way to undo said curse. For every power, there is an opposite power. Or, there is a way to destroy the power." Nemain gestured at me. "Take your gift, for instance, Clark. As far as I know, it cannot be destroyed. However, it can be blocked."

This entire conversation was beginning to make me nervous, and I had no idea why. This was all stuff that I'd understood for a very long time. There were two sides to every coin. It didn't always look the way you might expect. Not everything was always a direct reverse. Heads couldn't always be cancelled out by tails. But heads could still be cancelled out. Somehow.

"Balor Beimnech is not the only smiter in the history of the fae world," Nemain continued after she'd waited a moment for her words to sink in to my addled brain. "There have been a few others. They have always been in power. They have been conquerers. Some good. Some evil. But they have always used their eye to gain power, just like Balor has. It's always been difficult to stop them. But it's never been impossible. Lore tells us that there is a stone. The sling stone. And, when used, it destroys the smiter's eye."

I stared at Nemain, unblinking. My breath could barely escape my lungs. All I could do was repeat her words over and over in my mind, trying to make sense of them. Ancient lore. Ancient smiters. Destroyed because of a stone.

"You're lying," I said around a thick throat. "A magical stone can't destroy Balor's eye."

"Yes, it can," Moira said quietly. "I know, because I helped him hide it."

"If that's true, then why wouldn't you just destroy it? Why leave it out there in the world for someone to find?"

Moira sucked in a long, sorrowful breath. "Because whoever destroys it will die."

My eyes drifted to Duncan's body on the ground, and a sudden horrible realisation washed over me. Nemain wasn't making up stories. She wasn't telling me tall tales in order to manipulate me into doing something dumb. She had already done all that. She'd driven us here, waiting for us to do the one thing she couldn't do in order to destroy Balor. If she'd smashed the rock, she would have died.

So, instead, she'd tricked us into doing it ourselves.

Balor's eye was gone.

I needed to sit down.

The sling stone was the only thing in the world that could destroy Balor Beimnech's power. And Nemain had found a way to use it. The Crimson Court was well and truly fucked, and I had no idea how we were going to fix this.

Yep, definitely needed to sit down.

But there was nothing around us but rocks. Rocks I desperately did not want to touch now, not knowing if they held more terrible curses within them. I swallowed hard, doing my best to ignore the heavy pulsing of my heart.

"And the curse?" I asked in a shaky voice. "It had nothing to do with the sling stone, did it?"

A smile stretched across her face. "Of course it didn't. The Bullaun is not here. It isn't in your London ruins either."

"I don't suppose you're going to tell us where it is, huh?" Moira said.

"I mean, I could," Nemain replied, lacing her hands behind her back. "But that would be very silly of me, no? Sure, the main point of this plan was to destroy Balor's eye, but the curse is definitely a bonus. I actually considered not casting a curse at all. Of course, we needed a casualty to fully convince Balor it had been done. It took far more for him to trust you than I'd expected." A pause. "Everyone knows you two are…involved."

I narrowed my eyes. "You don't know a damn thing about my life."

"I know more than you think I do, Clark McCann."

"It. Is. Cavanaugh." Anger shook through me, making my head spin. My arms pulsed inside of my skin. If I wasn't careful, I would shift. And with my emotions heightened as they were, I would likely fall prey to the raven inside of me, blacking out again.

Now was definitely not a good time to lose consciousness.

"Careful, Clark," Ronan murmured, placing a strong and comforting hand on my back. "She's not worth it."

Nemain glanced from me to Ronan, back to me again. She tipped back her head and laughed. "Oh, I see what the problem is here. You've found yourself another male. That's why Balor doesn't trust you."

"I think we can probably move on to something more important than my love life," I said through gritted teeth. "Such as, where is the damn Bullaun, Nemain?"

"I am not going to tell you," she said crisply. "And I have no intention of handing it over to you."

"Everyone in House Beimnech will die. All those innocent fae." I shook my head, barely comprehending the truth of it. "Is that really what you want?"

"I will undo the curse. Just as soon as Balor is off that crimson throne." She flicked her fingers at the Fianna behind her. "But first, it's time for you three to die."

18

Nemain vanished through the trees as her Fianna warriors rushed toward the three of us. My sword was in my hands within seconds, the steel slicing through the rain-soaked air. Beside me, Moira did the same. Ronan's deep-throated growl shook through the clearing. He was halfway into his shift already. We just needed to keep the Fianna at bay long enough for him to fully become the wolf.

I raised my sword just in time. Steel slammed against steel. My entire body shook from the force of the blow, but I was swinging my blade despite the pain. The Fianna before me was tall and muscular, at least twice the size of me. That only meant he would be slower, not as quick on his feet.

He grinned as he jumped out of the way of my blow. With a roar, he lifted his sword high and slammed all of his weight behind it. It came straight down toward my head, the rain glinting off the blade.

I jumped to the side, heart in my throat. Despite all my training, I was still new to swordplay. This male had clearly been training all of his very long life. Likely for years, decades even.

Still, I knew I was fast. All I had to do was keep moving long enough for me to find my chance.

Ronan's roar ripped through the clearing. All the hair on the back of my neck stood on end as the wolfish creature pranced up to my side. He stood with his fangs only inches from my neck, his lips curled back as he growled at the fae who fought me.

The Fianna's face went white. He stumbled back, swallowing hard. Must have been the first time he'd come face-to-face with a wolf shifter. And he wasn't an idiot. Instead of facing the two of us combined, he turned tail and ran.

Ronan and I turned toward the next Fianna as if in unison. Together, we were practically unstoppable. Me with my blade, him with his fangs. It only took a few slashes by me and one big bite from him, and the warrior was on the ground, bleeding.

Moira had taken out the third. She stood over him with a blood-soaked blade, panting heavily. She wiped her face with the back of her arm, cleaned off her weapon, and slid it back into the sheath.

"Nemain got away," she said through laboured breaths. "She disappeared while we were fighting."

I turned to Ronan, wondering if he could understand my words while he was in wolf form. "Think you can catch up? We can't let her get away."

Ronan was off. He leapt through the air, his clawed feet pounding the forest ground. Moira and I waited in the clearing, doing our best to ignore the bodies, while Ronan went after Nemain. After what felt like hours, he finally returned.

"No luck," he said after shifting back into his human form. I tried not to drink in the sight of him, his perfectly-sculpted muscles, his…everything else. Quickly, he pulled on the clothes he'd shed before shifting. "I lost her scent halfway across the hills."

"Great," I said dryly. "So, this mission has been a disaster."

Moira blinked back her tears as we all glanced down at Duncan's prone form. "We're going to have to leave him here for now. We need to get back to London, warn Balor."

"I'll carry him," Ronan said quietly.

"We can't take him," Moira said, brushing aside a stray tear from her cheek. "We have to go back on the ferry, and there's no way to smuggle him on board there. And we can't risk the humans finding us with a dead body. That will only make this situation even worse. We're going to have to leave him. We have no other choice."

"What if we bury him?" I asked suddenly. "It won't be a deep grave, but at least it's better than leaving him out here on the forest floor."

Moira stared down at Duncan for a long moment before finally nodding. "Fine. But I need to call Balor while we're digging."

Ronan took up the first digging shift while Moira and I made the call to Balor. Neither of us were looking forward to filling him in on what had happened, but he was certain to know at least something had. If Nemain was telling the truth, his eye would be no more. My gut twisted just thinking about it. He was alone. None of us were there with him.

He was probably freaking the hell out.

It took five tries before he finally picked up the line. Moira spoke quietly into her cell, her words too low for me to hear. After a moment, she turned to me and held out the phone.

"You need to speak to him. I'm not having any luck."

My heart thumped hard as she slid the phone into my open palm. I held it up to my ear, waited, and then tried to find the right words. "Balor. Listen. We're going to find a way to fix this."

"I'm sure you believe that, Clark." His voice sounded super weird through the phone, as if he'd fallen into a deep well that he would never be able to escape. There was no emotion in his voice. Just a deadly kind of emptiness.

"Of course I believe that. There will be a way to get your power back. There always is."

"I am afraid that for once you are wrong."

"Magic always exists as a coin. On one side is your power. On the other is the sling stone. We can get it back by finding the opposite of the stone."

He let out a bitter chuckle. "The opposite of the sling stone *is* my power. And my power is gone. So is the sling stone, according to Moira. It's over, Clark."

"It's not over." I gripped the phone tighter in my hand and willed him to have a hope. Balor Beimnech could not give up. He was the Prince of the Crimson Court and Nemain's biggest rival. The only way the Court could survive was if he refused to give up.

But he didn't give me a chance to say any more. A click sounded in my ear. He'd hung up.

19

I knocked on the door of Balor's downstairs office where he spent most of his hours pouring over the boring paperwork of keeping over a hundred fae happy, safe, and in legal good standing with the human authorities. There were mouths to feed, electricity to keep humming along, and plenty more details I couldn't even imagine dealing with on a day to day basis.

No one truly knew how hard he worked, which was a testament to how good he was at the job.

All they truly noticed was his outward display of strength. His physicality. His overwhelmingly powerful presence. As long as that was intact, they were safe.

And Nemain had now destroyed that.

"This is not a good time, Clark." His voice sounded strained, and I didn't have to read his mind or scent his feelings to know that he was struggling beneath the weight of what had happened. Luckily, I wasn't actually a member of his Court anymore, so I didn't have to obey his commands. I cracked open the door and pushed inside.

Immediately, I was struck by the scent of booze. It clung to every wall in the room, hanging like a thick fog before me. The worst of it was coming from Balor. He was lounging back in his chair, free eye heavily lidded. His feet were kicked up on the desk before him, and his hands were awkwardly hanging like two dead weights.

"Go away," he said in a slur. "You're only going to make it worse."

"You're drunk." I perched on the edge of the leather guest chair and eyed him carefully. I'd never seen him like this. His carefully constructed persona made sure of that. He had to be the hard, always put together Prince of the Court. Never show too much emotion, unless it was disdain.

"What gives you that bright idea?" He chuckled and waved at his bar. It was a mess. There were about five open bottles, in every kind of liquor imaginable. Normally, he was on the whiskey, but I guessed tonight he didn't much care what he drank as long as it meant his mind could be numbed from the horrors of life.

"We need to talk," I said. "About…what happened."

"You mean my eye." He poked at the black eye patch he'd still chosen to wear, despite the fact that… well, I guessed he didn't need it anymore. It was weird to imagine him without it. The patch had become a part of his face to me. Of course, I wasn't about to say that out loud and make him feel worse about the whole thing.

"Unfortunately, it's not something we can really

ignore," I said, trying to pick my words carefully. "There will be some…repercussions."

It wasn't like I needed to tell Balor that. Clearly, he knew better than most exactly how terrible those repercussions might be.

"They'll all come for my crown. Hell, my entire Court might rebel against me. I'm nothing anymore. After everything I've done, after everything I've sacrificed, my damn eye will be the thing that damns me."

He slumped further into his chair.

I pursed my lips and stood. "Just hold onto that thought. I'll be back in a minute."

When I returned to Balor's office, I handed him a large cup of black coffee to sober him up a little. His metabolism was much faster than a human's (and mine), so it wouldn't take long before the effects would begin to wear off with the help of some caffeine. His eyebrows drifted to the top of his head, but he didn't turn down the hot liquid.

He took a big gulp, and then placed the mug on a glass coaster on his desk. "Don't look at me like that. I don't like it."

"I'm not looking at you any sort of way, Balor."

"You are." He leaned forward on his elbows, a bit of that spark coming back into his single visible eye. "It's an 'I feel sorry for you' kind of look. And it's not the kind of look the Prince of a Court should ever see."

In any other circumstance, I might argue with him. Balor firmly believed that vulnerability was a weakness. He'd spent his entire life carving out a certain image of himself, one of a shard of icy glass that no one could ever break. He thought that showing a softer side of himself would open himself up to being taken down by his enemies. The prophecy about his death for love probably hadn't helped.

But he was wrong. At least, normally he was. The fact his most powerful weapon was now gone truly was a…negative development.

"If I felt sorry for you, I'd be handing you more booze instead of a sobering cup of coffee. Drink your woes away and all that fun stuff." I shrugged. "Instead, I'm going to give you a bit of tough love. Sober the fuck up, Balor. Your Court depends on it."

"On my sobriety?" He lifted a brow and chuckled. "Sometimes, I forget how very human and idealistic you can be, Clark."

"I'm not being idealistic. I'm—"

He waved for me to stop. "My time as Prince of the Crimson Court has come to an end. No one ever dared present me with a full-on attack before. Why? I can take on any army single-handedly. Nemain no longer has to worry about that. She's taken out my eye, she's taken out two of my strongest warriors, and the rest of my Court will soon follow unless she does something to undo the curse."

"We'll find the other cursing stone."

"No." He shook his head. "It won't be anywhere that anyone can find. She's smarter than that."

I placed my palms flat on the table and leaned forward. "You need to snap out of this. It's not over until it's over. There's still a chance we can win this thing."

"We." He let out a bitter laugh and shook his head. "You're still saying that after all this?"

"Of course I am." I pushed up from the chair and

stalked toward him. "Why do you think I went to Ireland? Why do you think I've been running around London, trying to prove myself to you? And it's not just because of how I feel about you. It's not just because I—"

I cut myself off and moved away. The words got stuck in my throat. I couldn't bring myself to tell him, never mind that it was the worst timing I could have found. He was a mess. The Court was a mess. Hell, I was a mess, too, worry pulsing through my veins.

"Not just because you what, Clark?" The slurring was gone now. Instead, it had been replaced by the cool, measured steel I'd come to know. And love. He pushed up from his chair as I turned back toward him, his single red eye glittering with danger.

Balor strode toward me, his powerful body towering over mine. And, even though Nemain had destroyed the magic of his eye, power still curled off his body like tender, welcoming fingers that caressed at every inch of my exposed skin. I breathed it in deeply, leaning into it, savouring every single touch as if it would be the last.

Maybe it would be.

"You wouldn't feel that way if you saw the truth of what I am now." He lifted his hand to his eye patch, and flipped it up. The truth of him stood before me now. He'd never looked at me like this, with two full eyes gazing down at me. He couldn't now either, and it took all my self control not to show him how horrified I truly was. Where his flaming eye had once been was now a blackened hole of nothing.

I placed a hand to my lips, gasped. And then the

eye patch flipped back down on top of the blackened husk of power.

"So, you see," Balor said in a measured tone. "Now you know what I have become."

"Balor," I whispered, reaching up to touch his face. "You haven't become anything else. You're still the same fae. You're still the Prince."

He ground his teeth together and looked away. "How could you want someone whose biggest power now looks like this? How could you ever serve them?"

"Do you really not know?" I asked. "You are more than just your power."

"It's more complicated than that."

"Is it?" I arched a brow. "Was it my mind-reading power that made you…want me to fight by your side?"

His gaze went sharp. "Of course not."

"Of course not."

His lips twitched ever so slightly, just enough to make me hope that all was not yet lost. But then the smile fell again, and sorrow filled his eye. "I do not know what to do, Clark. I have never been more lost in my life. Not even when…"

He didn't finish his thought. He didn't need to. I could fill it in well enough on my own. Back when my parents had killed his sister, he'd known exactly what to do. Vengeance had been the only thing on his mind, but vengeance wouldn't help him now. We needed a plan. We needed to be strategic. We needed to show that Balor was still the same Prince he'd always been and that threatening his Court would get Nemain nowhere.

"It seems like it might be time to prepare for a

war." I gave him a sad smile. "But we have warriors. And the vamps and shifters will fight by our side."

Balor gave a heavy sigh and shook his head. "Our alliance with the shifters is quickly deteriorating. Several smaller Packs have broken off from the main one, and they want independence and nothing to do with any fae or vamps. Anderson is losing control of his people, and he's threatening to break himself free completely in order to regain control."

Ah, so it was worse than I'd thought. "And talking to them did nothing?"

"He is in a difficult situation. I can hardly blame him. His shifters are his first priority. Infighting has begun. If it continues, there may be casualties."

"Maybe I can talk to them."

Balor lifted a brow. "And what would you say?"

"The truth." I leaned forward and stared deeply into his eye. "That Nemain is a murderous tyrant and that you are not. That if he keeps himself out of this fight and she wins, then his life, as well as the lives of his Pack, will be in danger. He's better off with you in charge. And he knows that, or he wouldn't have allied himself with you in the first place."

He stared at me for a long moment before answering. "Are you still doing all of this to prove that you belong in this Court?"

"No." I strode over to the door and yanked it open. "I think I've more than proven my worth. If you don't see that, then that's on you."

20

My saucy exit from Balor's office lost some of its effect when I returned only ten minutes later with Ronan in tow. Still, I'd said what I'd wanted to say. As much as I wanted to be a part of his Court, and as much as I wanted him to forgive me for the part I'd played in his sister's death, I'd realised it was time I stopped beating myself up.

And he needed to get the hell over it, too.

"Ronan," I said, motioning to Balor. "Balor."

Ronan crossed his arms over his chest and choked out a laugh. "Yes, we've met, Clark. Many times."

Heat flushed into my cheeks. "I was just trying to make it all official-like."

In fact, as far as I could remember, we'd only ever all been together inside of or nearby Ronan's warehouse. This was the first time he'd stepped so firmly inside of Balor's world, and I could tell he was about as relaxed in here as he would be in a vat of lava. His skin was doing his signature Ronan thing where it looked like it was two seconds away from jumping off his body and hightailing it on out of here.

"Clark tells me you're having a shifter problem," Ronan said after a few tense and uncomfortable moments had passed.

"It's likely the same shifter problem you're having, I imagine." Balor moved over to his bar and pointed at the opened bottles. "A drink?"

Ronan visibly relaxed and gave a nod. "Please. Beer, if you have it."

Balor did not have beer. Instead, he poured Ronan two fingers of whiskey and handed it over before doing the same for himself. He didn't even have to ask me for my drink of choice. A refreshing gin and tonic came my way next. Then, we all settled into the chairs surrounding Balor's desk. He was starting to look more like himself again, now that we were making plans and talking strategies about how to tackle our enemies. Whatever drunken stupor had overtaken him had completely disappeared.

"I've got some rogue shifters forming their own packs out there and starting fights. Not just with each other but with my fae as well. And some humans."

Ronan's eyebrows winged upwards. "With humans?"

"That shocks you, but not the rest?"

"Some rogues had a go at me. I'm not sure if Clark told you." Ronan glanced my way. In fact, I had not yet told Balor. The chance hadn't come up, but now was as good as any. Quickly, we told the story, leaving out the part where we both got naked and almost had sex before I couldn't stop thinking about the damn fae Prince who didn't want me. With every moment that passed, Balor's face grew more and more tense.

"And this group spoke directly of Nemain?" Balor asked when we'd finished explaining what had happened that night.

"They made it abundantly clear that she'd given them the idea to attack us. They also seemed to think they would be protected by her now that they'd broken away from the Pack." Ronan's expression grew grim. "It seemed she wanted them to attack me in particular. I'm assuming because I've been helping Clark."

Balor's eyes drifted my way. "She does seem to have an intent focus on Clark."

"She's pissed off she can't manipulate me into helping her," I said matter-of-factly. "She had me under her thumb once before, and now she doesn't. She hates that."

"Maybe it isn't a good idea to send you out there," Balor mused, concern flickering in his eye.

"Send you out where?" Ronan asked.

"We need to go talk to the Pack," I explained. "Nemain will no doubt attack the Court any day now. Without the Pack's help…"

Realisation dawned in Ronan's eyes. "You want me to go with you and convince the Pack to fight Balor's war with him."

"Maybe."

Ronan let out a heavy sigh.

"*My* war," Balor said with narrowed eyes, "is the same war that every supernatural in London should be concerned with."

"You're fighting for your throne, for your power," Ronan countered. "You want to keep your crown."

"Yes," Balor replied matter-of-factly. "And do you know why I want to keep my crown instead of give it up to Nemain? Because she is violence personified. Anyone who does not wholeheartedly support her is an enemy. She sees vampires and shifters as Other, lesser beings that need to be stomped out. If she were some kind of noble, honourable fae who had truly done great things in her life for others, then this might be a different conversation."

A beat passed before Ronan replied. "What makes you think I'll agree to do this?"

Balor turned my way, his single visible eye zeroing in on me. "For the same reason you went to Ireland to track down the Bullaun. Clark will go and speak to the Pack, regardless of what you or I say. She shouldn't go alone. She needs backup. You'll do it for her, if for nothing else."

My heart pounded in my ears as the two males stared each other down. Testosterone rippled through the air, sucking all the breath from my lungs. Their expressions were hard; their bodies tense. They were about to punch the shit out of each other, or worse.

Finally, the tension released its tight grip on Ronan's shoulders. He slumped back into the chair and shook his head. "Dammit all to hell."

"I need to ask you something, and I need for you to answer me honestly," Ronan said as we strode down the front steps of the Crimson Court.

Never a good statement to hear. From anyone.

"I'll answer honestly if I can answer honestly. That's all I can promise you," I decided to say.

"You and Balor seem to be over your little row. He's welcomed you back into the fold, even if not officially."

"Yeah, you're not wrong there." I gave a nod. "But that seems more like a statement than a question."

"The question's coming," he said gruffly. He stopped suddenly. "Are you two an item now? Are you sleeping together again?"

I sucked in a deep breath and pressed my lips together. "No."

He arched a brow. "No? That isn't much of an explanation."

"You asked a question. I answered it honestly."

"So, you aren't going to start sleeping with him again?"

"Definitely not," I said. "Partly because we were never sleeping together in the first place."

Ronan crossed his arms over his chest and gave me a frank look. "Don't lie, Clark. Not to me."

"Okay, you want honesty? I'll give you honesty. But I'm going to warn you. You're probably going to wish I'd kept my mouth shut."

When he didn't reply, I was forced to continue. "Balor and I are not an item. We never have been. We never will be either."

He opened his mouth to speak, but I held up a hand and shook my head. "Do I wish things were different? Yes. A million times yes. I don't know how to explain it. There's no logic when it comes to how I feel about that fae. He makes me feel…I don't know, alive, or something. Like I am more me than I am when I'm not around him. Like a part of my soul resides in him, and he in me. It doesn't make sense, and I've tried to ignore it, but I can't. If you want to know why I've pushed you away, that's it."

Ronan stared at me for a long while before letting out a long, tired sigh. "I understand. You've made yourself more than clear."

As we strode down the street, I was momentarily distracted from our horrible conversation by a round of shouts peppering the air. I slowed to a stop to find a crowd of humans gathered outside on the Crimson Court's front lawn. There were about a hundred of them, maybe more. They were all holding signs, waving them high as we passed.

"No more magic! No more fae!" a girl in front shouted, pointing a finger at me.

"No more vamps! No more beasts!" they continued. "No more magic! No more fae!"

I turned to Ronan with raised brows. "Well, this is certainly an interesting development."

"Not an unexpected one though," he said with a frown as we moved away from the jeering crowd. "The humans have been getting restless about us for awhile. I guess this means they've snapped."

Definitely not unexpected. And definitely unwanted.

I cast one last glance over my shoulder at the chanting humans. We had enough trouble without worrying about humans. The fae were ripping themselves apart, the vamps were restless themselves, and the shifters…well, I guessed we'd find out soon where the shifters stood.

I had a feeling I wasn't going to like what we'd find.

21

When we reached the home of the Pack, I started to understand why Ronan was the way he was. We stood in front of a bank of old warehouses, situated on the edge of the river as far east in London as one could go before it stopped being London. There was a tube stop a few blocks away, but Ronan told me it had closed down years ago.

Graffiti covered the metal walls and motorbikes decorated the gravel lawn. Several shifters were lounging around outside, toasting beer bottles and hovering around a bin that was lit up with flames. Thumping bass echoed from inside the nearest warehouse, electric guitars drifting out through the cracks.

"Welcome to the home of the Pack," he said, gesturing at the scene before us. "Now you know why I left."

I scanned the grounds again, drinking in the easy camaraderie, the relaxed poses of the men, women, and children running through the gravel with carefree abandon. "I don't know. Doesn't look so bad to me."

"Trust me. When you live deep inside of this mess, you want nothing more than to get out. Everyone is smiling. Underneath it all, there's brawls and drama and so much talking shite that it makes your head spin."

"That just sounds like life, Ronan."

"Which is why I live alone."

"Why you *used to* live alone," I reminded him as we strode into the open door of the warehouse. "You're not getting rid of me that easily."

"There you're wrong," he said, expression going dark. "Balor will take you back. He'd be an idiot not to."

My heart thumped as I glanced up at him. I guessed our earlier conversation was still on his mind. I'd said far too much about my bond with Balor. So much that I wished I could rewind time and take it back.

"Listen," I started to say, trying to find the words to explain myself.

He stopped, held up a hand. "Don't, Clark. There's no need. I get how things are just fine."

Without another word, he continued to move across the warehouse. For a moment, I stared after him. His strong back rippled beneath his tight black shirt. His gate was smooth and confident, full of power. God, I was an idiot. Why couldn't I just be a normal girl who wanted a normal boy?

He'd made it halfway across the floor before I finally caught up with him. Ronan was making a beeline for the back left corner where several familiar figures were clustered around a pool table. Anderson, the Pack member I'd ran into during that whole Circle of Night business. He hadn't been in charge then, but he'd somehow fought his way to the top after that.

He gave off the aura of an alpha. Pure power rippled off his body. He was a powerful shifter, and now he was in charge. And I knew he had a soft spot for me, since I'd delivered some murderous vamps to his doorstep.

"What can I do for you, Clark?" Anderson asked, shooting me a grin as he put down his pool stick and ambled over. "It's not every day we get a fancy fae visitor."

"I came here to talk to you about your alliance with the Crimson Court."

The smile slipped from his lips. "Damn. I thought you'd broken free of that Court. Can't say I'm too surprised you went back. You and the Prince seemed pretty close back then."

Ronan shot me a look. One that I promptly ignored.

"I'm not really here in an official capacity or anything. I'm here because I'm worried about the supernaturals of London. That includes you and your Pack."

He sighed and leaned against the pool table. "I'm going to tell you exactly what I told Balor. I appreciate the alliance. I always have. But my Pack is better off extracting itself from this mess while we still have the chance to do it. If I don't do this for them, I don't think we'll ever come back from it."

"I'm sure you know who Princess Nemain is," I said.

He gave a slow nod. "I do. She's the one making a mess out of the whole thing. I know. And I don't approve. That doesn't mean I can do a damn thing to stop her."

"You can fight by Balor's side when she attacks. That's what you can do."

"And now, this is where I'm going to turn your words right back onto you." His eyes glittered. "I'm sure you know about the rogues."

"Yes. Ronan and I were attacked by a group of them."

"Then, you'll know my current predicament. The number of rogues are growing. They're refusing to stop fighting until I take the Pack out of the alliance. So, that's what I've done. I'll be honest, I do care about the fae. I'd like to stick to what I promised your Prince. But much like your Prince, I have to think about my people first. Their lives are at stake here, Clark. I've gotta get us out before it's too late."

I blew out a hot breath and tried to find the words to disagree with the leader of the shifters. Problem was, they weren't there in my brain. I understood his point far better than I wanted to admit. He needed to protect his people. Just like we had to protect ours.

"You're leaving, aren't you?" Ronan asked from beside me.

Eyes wide, I twisted back toward the shifter, who was giving a slow nod. "The Fianna are on their way to attack London. They said that any shifter found out on the streets would be at risk of being attacked, because the Fianna will just assume they're on Balor's side. On top of that, the humans are getting restless in this city. We're going to go somewhere more peaceful, without all the supernatural wars."

My cheeks flamed. "You can't just leave London."

"Fuck London," Anderson said. "We're done here."

22

"So, that didn't go well," I muttered to Ronan as we lurked in the corner of the warehouse. Now that I knew the truth about what the Pack intended to do, the makeshift party before me transformed into something much different. There were a lot of high-fives and reminiscing. Photos were being passed around.

This was a goodbye party, their last hurrah in the city before they got the hell out.

"I know you're wondering if there's something else you can do to get them to stay. But there isn't." Ronan's hooded gaze spread across the party. "They're stubborn. And when it comes down to it, when the pack is in danger, they rally around each other, shove everyone else out."

"At least we still have the vampires," I muttered, sure to keep my voice quiet enough so that the shifters wouldn't hear the words.

Ronan shifted my way with a strange expression on his face. He opened his mouth to speak, but a loud crash of exploding glass cut through the moment. In unison, we whirled toward the sound. The small windows lining the front wall of the warehouse were gone, glass sprinkling the steel-grey cement floor.

My hand found my sword just as a dozen Fianna leapt through the cracked openings. They landed with speed and grace, one hand holding them steady as they crouched before us.

"I guess they didn't want to wait for the shifters to leave," Ronan muttered beneath his breath. "Should have figured."

I curled my fingers around the hilt of my sword, narrowing my eyes. "Nemain cannot be trusted. She won't stop until every single one of her enemies is dead. That includes shifters. Vamps, too."

"Well, I'm not going to let them destroy this Pack." He leapt into the air. Halfway there, his body transformed into the powerful beast that lived within him. He was all fur and claws, fangs bared as he joined his fellow shifters in the fight.

I raced forward with my sword, mentally calling out for the ravens in the skies. My feet stopped short when a Fianna appeared before me. She was tall and thin, body carved like a powerful Greek statue. She grinned, her teeth glittering along with her sword.

"We had no idea you'd be here." Her smile widened. "I can't wait to tell Nemain that I personally took out her greatest enemy."

I snorted, narrowing my eyes. "Problem is, I don't know how you're going to be able to tell her a damn thing when you're six feet under."

An animalistic cry tore from her throat, and she launched into battle. I brought my sword up fast, clanging hard against the force of her blow. We traded swings, our swordplay matched evenly. I got one swing at her. She blocked it. She got a swing at me. I managed to throw my sword up just in time. On and on it went like this for what felt like hours.

"Give. Up!" She screamed as she pushed her sword against mine. I stumbled back, gritting my teeth as a new wave of anger and fear poured through me. My ravens hadn't appeared, but I'd been so focused on the one-to-one battle that I hadn't been able to call out long enough to find them in the skies.

Her blade swung out fierce and hard once again. With a deep breath, I jumped. This time, I didn't try to dodge the attack. I leaned into it, grabbing ahold of the weapon's sharp edge with the palm of my hand. Her eyes opened wide when I ripped the sword right out of her hands.

Pain lanced through my fingers; blood dripped on the floor.

But now she was no longer armed.

I stabbed my blade right into her heart and twisted hard. The life left her eyes almost immediately. With horror churning through my gut, I yanked the blade out of her chest and whirled toward the fight.

Carnage was everywhere.

Blood painted the walls.

With a deep breath, I tipped back my head and wailed, crying out for the help of my birds. Magic shot from my throat as a strange, eerie song filled the air. Wind whipped around me, slapping my face with my hair. A tornado of power swarmed around my body. It swallowed me whole.

Slowly, I managed to snap my jaws shut, gulping down the cry of rage.

An eerie silence filled the air. The fighting had stopped. Every Fianna in the room had dropped dead. The only ones left standing were the wolves. And they were all looking right at me, as if staring straight into my soul.

23

"I've done everything I can to help you," Ronan said as he threw another t-shirt into his duffel bag. "The Fianna are going to continue attacking, and there aren't enough of us to make a difference. I'm afraid it's time to give up, Clark."

"I can't believe you're saying this," I said, watching him toss another shirt onto the pile. "You're a fighter. You're not a runner."

After the weird wailing moment in the Pack's headquarters, Anderson and his fellow shifters, the ones left alive, had quickly made a hasty exit from their home. They grabbed their bags, their motorbikes, and hightailed it on out of there. Ronan had wanted to come straight back home. Apparently, he wanted to do the same damn thing they had.

He paused for a moment before shaking his head. "And that's where you're wrong, Clark. How do you think I survived the attack on my Pack? I ran. I got the hell out. And I'm going to get the hell out again. I'm not ready to die, especially not to some arsehole fae who think they're better than I am."

And not *for* some arsehole fae either, I couldn't help but think.

"So, you're going with Anderson's Pack now, after renouncing him over and over and over again. What happened to independence? What happened to being your own man?"

He stopped suddenly, turning to face me with a fierce look in his eye. "How can I be my own man if I'm dead?"

My heart thumped hard. "Come on. You're one of the strongest shifters I've ever met. Your wolf is a force of nature. It'll take a hell of a lot for the Fianna to kill you."

He whirled toward me, eyes wild. "Did you not see what they did to the Pack? I know those shifters. They're just as strong as I am, Clark. Some of them even more so. The Fianna have been training for these kinds of battles all their lives. It's how they took out my whole damn Pack, too. They're not going to stop. They're going to keep coming. And I'm not going to be here when they do. Whatever magic you just did back there…it somehow worked. But you don't even know how you did it. There's no guarantee you'd be able to do it again"

I didn't really know what to say to that. He was right, of course. The Fianna would keep coming. And they would win, unless there were enough fighters out there trying to stop them.

Losing Ronan felt like losing the war.

I pressed my lips together. "I don't want to say goodbye to you."

His expression softened. "I don't want to say goodbye to you either. I'm not much of a fan of flatmates, but you've been alright. Hell, I've kind of enjoyed the company."

"Please don't leave," I said in a soft whisper. "I've lost a lot of people over the years. I really don't want to lose another."

"Then, come with me, Clark." He grabbed my bag and tossed it my way. "Pack your things. We can get out of this hellhole of a city, go somewhere that isn't steeped in fights day by day. Somewhere quiet. Somewhere calmer. Somewhere without power hungry supes."

I shook my head, unable to say a word.

"I know I've just been a roof over your head and a bed underneath your head, but I promise that we can have a nice life."

"I can't," I whispered, holding back the tears. "You've been far more than just a roof over my head, Ronan, but I can't bear to leave the Court behind."

"And yet you say there's nothing going on between the two of you." He shook his head. "You'll stay in a burning city just for him. Just for Balor. And you can't even tell me the truth about it."

"Because there isn't anything going on between us. I know that's hard for you to believe, but it's the truth." I grabbed his arm and forced him to stop. "Yes, I'm staying for him, but I'm also *not* staying for him. This is about far more than Balor Beimnech. I feel a sense of loyalty to the Court that I can't explain. I certainly never expected it. Hell, I didn't even want to join them at first." I shook my head, trying to find a way to express the emotions churning through me.

"They're mine. And I'm theirs. I have to help them. I don't know how I can make a lick of difference, but I can't leave them to fight this battle alone."

Ronan's eyes softened, and he gave a nod of understanding. "They're your Pack. You've just explained how it feels to have a Pack. Somehow, through all this mess, you've found them."

My heart beat hard inside of me. I hadn't understood the truth of it until now, and if Ronan hadn't spoken the words, I might never have. Even though I'd always considered myself a fae and not a shifter, I couldn't ignore the fact that I was both. And the shifter side of me had sprung to life these past few months. It was awake inside of me, breathing and wanting and yearning for a conspiracy of ravens to call my own. But the birds of the sky were not mine.

My Pack was the Crimson Court.

A shifter would do anything for her Pack.

And that was me.

24

Halfway back to the Court, the attacks throughout the city started. The sirens were the first thing that tipped me off. And then it was the screaming, the crying, and the plumes of smoke that drifted up between the closely-packed buildings of the city skyline. I ran through the maze of streets, passing screaming humans who held their children tight in their arms.

By the time I reached the Court, I'd seen at least half a dozen bodies on the ground. All were human. All were dead. I'd stopped when I first saw them, thinking I could make some kind of difference, hoping that my powers could help them somehow.

But I could not bring people back from the dead. The only way I could help the humans was by putting a stop to Nemain's reign of terror before it truly began.

I reached the front steps of the Court just in time to see the group of protesting humans had grown from a hundred to almost a thousand. They were packed tight on the lawn, waving their hand-made signs as high as they could. Their coordinated chants had transformed into screams. They could see the distant smoke on the horizon. The attacks were being reported all over social media.

And they blamed the fae.

Hell, I did, too. Nemain was behind this, which meant this was *our* fault. Humans were dying from faerie attacks. London would never be the same after this.

When I reached the bottom of the stairs, I glanced up to see Moira throw open the door. She waved for me to hurry, her eyes flicking toward the growing crowd. She was nervous. I could tell by the slight twitch above her left eye. It would only take a single spark, and this protest could turn into a violent riot where people might die.

"She's using coordinated attacks throughout the city," Moira said when I joined her at the top of the stairs. "They all happened around the same time. About twenty in total, if the news is a good indicator of the damage."

I pressed my lips together. "Casualties?"

"They don't know yet." A pause. "Though the guess is well over a hundred."

My heart squeezed tight. Over a hundred innocent humans, dead because a sociopathic fae wanted a throne.

When we strode into the command station, Balor, Kyle, and Elise were waiting for us. It was strange not to see Duncan standing by the Prince's side, along with Cormac. They'd always been there, always present during emergencies to do whatever had to be done.

Elise and Kyle were clever, but the warriors were his fists, his swords. Moira was the best warrior Balor had left now. The only one on his team of guards.

We were fucked.

"Moira filled me in on the attacks," I began before Balor had a chance to say a word. "But I ran into a few of them myself. The Pack got attacked by Fianna while I was there. A few casualties. Most of them got out alive."

I flicked my gaze to Moira before glancing at Balor. That whole battle cry thing had been super weird, and I didn't know how it fit into either my shifter powers or my fae powers. It wasn't something I'd ever been able to do until now. Hell, maybe it had just been a fluke. A one-time thing I'd never be able to replicate.

Balor lifted a brow. "There's something you aren't saying."

Damn him and his scenting power. It was practically as useful as my own.

"The shifters won the battle because…well, because I shouted, basically." I shrugged. "My powers felt the same as they do whenever I'm about to shift, but the magic came pouring out of my mouth instead of transforming my skin."

Elise's eyes widened, and Moira let out a gasp. That was strange. Sure, a new, undiscovered power at the age of twenty-five wasn't exactly normal, but it wasn't that weird.

Balor's eye glittered as he gave me a long look from head to toe. "You gave a battle cry?"

"That's impossible," Moira said quickly, frowning as she glanced at me. "She's only half-fae. Besides… the Queen has been dead a very long time. She couldn't come back now. She could only pass her powers along directly. That's how her magic worked."

I turned toward Moira, frowning. "What the hell are you talking about?"

"We're talking about The Phantom Queen," she said frankly. "The Morrigan."

I coughed out a laugh and shook my head. "That's ridiculous. What does The Morrigan have to do with me?"

"I have long been wondering the very same thing, Clark," Balor said quietly.

I whirled to face him, heart hammering hard in my chest. "She doesn't have anything to do with me. Like Moira said, she's dead. And I'm half-fae. Just because I change into a raven doesn't mean I'm related to her at all."

"No, you're right," Moira said. "You aren't the only shifter who transforms into a raven. There are only a handful of animals that reside within a shifter's body, and that's one of them."

"It's the…other things that have made me wonder," Balor said. "She not only transforms into a raven, but she can call them. That is pure Morrigan. And now, the battle cry."

Moira pressed her lips firmly together. "I'll admit, it's odd."

"Holy shit," Kyle finally said, breaking through the conversation with wide eyes. He was staring at me, peeking out from underneath his mop of fiery hair, in a way he'd never looked at me before. Like I was a stranger, one who simultaneously intrigued him and terrified him. "She's the fucking Morrigan."

"I am *not* the Morrigan," I said.

"The battle cry is her unique power. No other fae can wield that kind of magic. The shifters won, right? It's because you were fighting by their side. You used your power to make them win. They're alive because of you."

My heart thumped hard. "I am only half-fae. And the Morrigan is one of the most powerful fae to have ever existed. That's certainly not me. You've seen me fight."

Balor's gaze was intense as he stared at me. I shifted on my feet, growing increasingly unnerved by the focus. As cool as it would be to think I was the most powerful fae alive, I certainly wasn't. Whatever they thought they saw in me, they were wrong. I'd never been particularly great at the whole fae thing. I was often weak. And a little bit clumsy. The Morrigan had never been any of those things. There were reasons her statues littered the grounds of this Court, as well as each of the other six Courts on this planet.

It was ridiculous to think I was anything like her.

"I appreciate the vote of confidence," I finally said, holding up my hands. "But I'm not the Morrigan. If I was, don't you think we'd be winning against Nemain right now?"

"She has a point," Moira said.

"That's not how it works," Kyle argued. "It isn't about strategy. It's about battle. On the field, that's where the Morrigan's power really counts."

Balor rubbed his chin. "Did Nemain hear the battle cry?"

"Nemain wasn't there," I said. "I assume she was busy with one of the other attacks she'd planned on London."

"Okay." Balor sucked in a deep breath. "That's good. If you truly are the Morrigan, she won't know."

I rolled my eyes. "Honestly, I'm not —"

Balor's cell phone rang. It sat in the center of the command station table, little lights beaming up like a beacon. The number on the display was blocked, so 'unknown' was the only word that scrolled across the screen.

We all turned to look at each other, matching grim expressions on our faces. Whatever this was, it wouldn't be good.

Balor snatched the phone off the table and pressed the speaker phone button. A familiar voice slithered out of the speaker before Balor even had a chance to speak.

"I believe you've gotten my warning," Nemain said breezily, her voice echoing throughout the lofted space of the command station. Balor visibly stiffened; Moira clenched her jaw. And I grabbed onto the edge of the table as tight as I could.

"Yes," Balor said in a calm and even tone of voice. "We did. You've made your point. Loud and clear. I assume you're headed here, to the Court, next."

She let out a tinkling laugh, and then her voice went razor sharp. "No, I don't think I will. Instead, I have something much more interesting to propose to you. See, I have some human prisoners now. Hostages, if you will. My Fianna are on the way back to House Futrail, with at least a dozen of these humans. They're alive, of course. For now."

"What are you playing at, Nemain?" Balor asked in a low growl.

"Give up your crown and your throne to me, and I will release the humans." A pause. "Or else every single one of them will die."

25

"Balor," I said, following him into his office after he'd stormed out of the command station. "Can we talk?"

His back stiffened, and he shot me a cold look over his shoulder. "You should leave."

My heart felt punched in the face, but I pressed on. "Look, I know Nemain has put you between a rock and a hard place, but we need to do something. She has humans, and she still has the cursing stone. Maybe if—"

"I am not giving her the throne. I will protect my fae until the final breath I take."

"I understand that. But there must be something we can do."

"Clark," he said in a low growl. "You need to go back home to Ronan. You've been banished. I let myself forget that, but it's not something I can ignore any longer. You need to leave, and you can never come back." He whirled to face me. "Do you understand?"

Tears filled my eyes. "If that's what you really want Balor, then I'll go."

His expression hardened into stone. "It's what I want."

~

"They're clearly planning something else," I said as I paced back and forth across the courtyard of the Crimson Court. The city had a strange energy, different than the usual pulse of life. A darkness had settled over London, and a strange hush peppered the air, shot through with the occasional song of sirens.

The Fianna had retreated. They could have come straight for Balor, but they hadn't. Wasn't that the whole point of taking his eye? So that they could attack without any worry he'd burn them all down?

Why hadn't they attacked? Why had they gone back home? Sure they'd taken some human hostages with them, but it didn't make much sense. It would have been much easier for them to come straight here.

Moira stood with her hand resting firmly on the hilt of her sword. Even though the threat was seemingly gone, she was still on edge. "It's more than a little odd."

"Nemain had the upper hand here. She's got the Fianna, she's chased away the shifters, and the vamps are nowhere to be seen." I would have to remember to punch Matteo in his stupid smug face the next time I saw him. "But instead of attacking, she took some humans as hostages and gave Balor an ultimatum. How does that make sense?"

Moira shook her head. "I don't know, and I don't like it."

I bit my bottom lip and paced back and forth across the damp grass in front of the many Morrigan statues. "We have to do something."

"Balor made his choice," Moira said quietly. "I don't know if there's much we can do."

I stopped before my friend, searching her eyes for evidence of what she hadn't spoken aloud. "Do you agree with him? His decision?"

"I think Balor is scared for the safety of his fae. Sure, she gave him a choice, but it wasn't much of one. He would never sacrifice the lives of his family for the lives of strangers. That's not Balor."

"So, we're just going to have to go save them ourselves. And find out what Nemain plans to do next."

"Any idea how we're going to do that?"

"Yeah, I have to sneak into House Futrail. I don't see any other way. I'll shift into the raven, fly there, and scope things out. Then, we can take things from there."

A deep frown pulled down Moira's lips. "That sounds a hell of a lot like you tackling this shit on your own."

"Do you have a better idea?" I asked.

Her expression grew darker. "No."

I gave a nod. "The raven it is."

My trip back up to Ireland went a hell of a lot faster than it had by car and boat. My wings spread wide as I swooped through the skies, breathing in the fresh air. Feathers ruffled all along my tiny body, reminding me of who and what I was.

I was the bird, and the bird was me. The only way to stay in control was to accept the animalistic part of myself and embrace it. The more I pushed it away, the more it wanted to come out and scream in rage. The bird didn't want to be pushed down.

She wanted to come out and play.

I reached the shores in record time and flew into a shop when no one was paying attention. After I'd transformed back into my human form, I stole some clothes. I wasn't proud of it, but I didn't have any other choice. If I wandered around the streets of Belfast in my birthday suit, I'd bring far too much unwanted attention onto myself.

I needed to be stealthy.

Unfortunately, Elise had been unable to cast a glamour over me. We'd made a couple of attempts, but the shift always threw off her magic, just like clothes.

House Futrail was located about half an hour outside of Belfast, a stone's throw away from the Giant's Causeway on the coast. It was a large house set up high beside the sea, its tall commanding form casting shadows on the rippling waters at the base of the cliff. From my view across the hills, it was dark and forbidding, like something out of an old gothic horror film.

With a deep breath, I peeled off my clothes once

again and left them hidden beneath a large rock. I needed to stake things out in raven form first, and find an unguarded entrance, if there was one.

Back in the skies once again, I circled the house once, twice, and then once more for good measure. I wasn't entirely sure what I'd expected before I came here, but this strange, eerie silence wasn't it. Where were all the warriors? Where were all the humans they'd captured to use as leverage over Balor? It almost looked as though nobody was home. No lights in the windows. No smoke curling out of the two large chimneys that sat on either end of the crooked roof.

Flapping my wings, I lowered myself to a windowsill to peer into the depths of the Fianna's home base. Instantly, the house transformed, as if a magic veil had suddenly slipped away to reveal the full truth beneath it. The place was a hive of activity, bright sparkling lights lit up in every window. Fianna were coming and going from a room that was packed to the brim with tables covered in so much food that my little bird stomach began to growl.

My beak twitching, I took to the skies again, and the dark, foreboding version of the House slithered back into view again.

Huh. That was interesting. I hadn't known that glamour could be applied to buildings as well as people. Something to keep in mind for later.

If there was a later.

I swooped down low to get close to each of the windows. Activity was abuzz in every room. When I came to a window at the very end of the second story, I spied Aed and several other Fianna undergoing a series of training moves that looked a lot like karate.

Weapons were piled high in one of the corners. They were preparing for something. Battle? If so, why had they left London when they'd had the perfect chance to attack?

I had to get inside and find out.

After several more moments of flying around the House like a lost puppy, I finally spotted an opening door on the eastern side, a female Fianna stepping out with a cigarette pack in her hand. Before I could miss my chance, I soared through the air and slid inside only a millisecond before the door slammed shut behind her.

I let out a long breath—long for a bird, anyway—and glanced around. Ideally, I'd shift back into my human form again. I was a lot more comfortable in my Clark skin, and much more accustomed to sneaking around with two feet instead of claws and wings.

But I could remain more unseen up here like this, silently flapping in the rafters. Plus, there was the whole clothes issue. Best not wander around House Futrail buck naked.

The door suddenly opened again before I'd had a chance to move forward. I froze. Kind of. My wings still had to beat at the air to keep me high in the ceiling instead of on the ground. As silent as I was, I was still making some noise. One look up, and they'd see me. Hopefully, they'd just shoo me away.

"Nemain's calling a meeting," the warrior said as she shut the door behind her. She had a cell phone pressed tightly against her ear, and a half-finished cigarette in the other hand. "Says it's urgent. There's a new development with the whole Crimson Court situation."

My ears pricked up. A meeting? A new development?

I hoped I wasn't too late.

The warrior paused in her steps, just below where I flapped crazily in the ceiling. She cocked her head and frowned at whatever her friend had said on the other line. "Yeah, it's got something to do with the McCann girl."

My heart thumped hard. What the hell was she talking about? Obviously, I was the McCann girl—as much as it pissed me off that Nemain insisted on calling me by the name I'd long since rejected—but that didn't make much sense. Why would she be having a meeting about me?

The warrior finally began to drift further down the hall, but her footsteps were far too slow for my liking. I'd been flailing in the air for a good ten minutes now, and my arms—er, wings—were beginning to tire. After the long flight here from London, and now this, the tiny bird that lived inside of me needed some rest.

"You just need to come, okay? Stop stalling. You know that if you don't join us, then she's going to come for your throne next."

Okay, now that was seriously alarming. If this Fianna was talking to someone with a throne, that meant she was working with another Prince or Princess of the Seven Courts. But who? I couldn't imagine many of them would be willing to side with Nemain, not after everything she'd done and especially not with everything she planned to do.

Had she given them some sort of promise? Or was she tricking them into allying themselves with her? She'd stretch out her arm to shake hands, and then she'd wrap that arm around her enemy and stab them in the back.

Suddenly, the warrior stiffened and dropped back her head. Her eyes zeroed in on me. And then she glanced back down. "I've gotta go. A bird has gotten into the House. Yes, a bird."

But I didn't stick around to hear the end of her conversation. Whether or not she thought I was an actual bird didn't matter. I didn't want to be there when she decided she wanted to try and get me out of here.

Slowly, I made my way from the ground floor up to the next where I thought I'd spied Aed and the others training for their upcoming mission. But when I reached the room, there was no one inside. The weapons were still piled up in the corner, but the trainees had vanished into thin air. Another glamour? Or had they rushed into the meeting with Nemain?

I had to find that damn meeting. If I were going to get some answers today, it would be there.

The bird within me began to pulse against my brain. I shuddered and closed my eyes, trying my hardest to hang on to Clark instead of letting the raven take full control over my mind. Now was really not a good time for me to lose consciousness. It might be my only chance to get information.

After several long, agonising moments passed, I shook off the bird and turned my attention back onto the hallway outside of the training room. I listened carefully, calling upon my enhanced raven senses to find what I was looking for.

There, just a few doors down, I heard the unmistakable sound of murmuring voices. One of those voices was terrifyingly familiar. Nemain was here. She'd started her meeting. And I had to get as close to her as I could possibly bring myself. Even after all this time, and even in my shifted form, slivers of fear still went through me at the thought of her.

Slowly, I edged down the hallway, closer and closer to the room where Nemain was holding court. The door had been left cracked open, just enough for me to catch the words being spoken.

"As you know, Clark McCann has been making our mission far more unbearable than it should be." A pause. "However, all of that is about to change. We can use her now to get exactly what we need in order to take control of the Crimson Court."

I tried to frown around the raven beak. What the hell was she talking about? Use me to get the crown? It made no sense. I would never help her, let alone hand her that stupid throne made of crimson skulls. She must be far more delusional than I originally thought.

I inched a little closer to the door so that I could better hear the conversation.

And that was when everything was plunged into darkness.

26

I woke up in a jail cell with my clothes piled by my side, the ones I'd left beneath a rock outside. Well, it was more of a dungeon than a jail. The ground was covered in dirt, and the walls were yellowed and rotting. Without any windows on the walls, it was tough to see through the thick shadows that permeated everything. But the flickering torches lining the wall illuminated enough for me to know that I was stuck underground.

At the far end of the long and skinny corridor, a warrior—the female I'd spotted taking a smoke break—stood outside of a large, wooden door. That must be the exit of this place.

She cast a glance my way and noted that I'd begun to stir. She quickly disappeared behind the door. Only moments passed before she returned.

"I don't suppose I could tempt you into letting me go?" I called out to her as I finished pulling on my stolen clothes. Obviously, I expected nothing of the sort, but I was hoping I could get a few tidbits of information out of her.

For one, where the hell was I? And two, what exactly did Nemain intend to do with me?

"Nemain is my Queen. I follow her orders," the warrior said in a crisp voice. "Her orders are to not let you go under any circumstances whatsoever. And that includes you falling ill."

My eyebrows shot to the top of my forehead. "Queen? That's new. Last time I checked, she was the Princess of the Silver Court and nothing more."

"She is Queen of Faerie," the warrior said. "She rules us all."

My heart beat harder in my chest. Even though Nemain was yet to win another crown, she already had her lackeys calling her their Queen. "There hasn't been a Queen of Faerie in a very long time."

"Not since the last Phantom Queen," the Fianna said. "And it's time that changed."

I frowned. The Phantom Queen, or the lack thereof, had nothing to do with this. Not unless Nemain was somehow convinced that she was the next reincarnation of the Morrigan. When she'd been alive, she'd often been the one who ended up on the throne. The fae prospered when she reigned. They felt safe. They felt protected. No one could harm them as long as the Morrigan was in charge.

But, in the end, she'd abandoned Faerie once and for all.

"I heard you talking on the phone earlier," I said, deciding to take a different approach. There had to be a reason that this warrior was following Nemain, one steeped in some kind of logic. If I could somehow counter that logic by showing her a different side of things, maybe she wouldn't be so quick to follow a murderous sociopath.

The warrior frowned. "I thought that was you up there in the ceiling. Bit weird, your bird thing."

"You're not wrong about that," I said with a slight smile. "I'm still trying to get used to the whole thing myself. It's only been a few weeks that I've been shifting."

She shifted on her feet, taking the smallest of steps closer to my cell. "Didn't you know you were half of a shifter?"

"I did. But my father wasn't around to talk me through it. I never really knew how to shift. Didn't really want to either, to be honest."

"Huh. Well, looks like you've gotten the hang of it pretty quickly."

"Not quickly enough." I gestured at the metal bars surrounding me. "Otherwise, I wouldn't have gotten caught."

"You probably wouldn't have gotten caught if Nemain hadn't known you were coming." She smiled at the look of shock that flittered across my face. "It was a little bit of a trap, to be honest. She hoped you'd be tempted to come here when you found out we retreated from London."

I fought the urge to scowl. "And why the hell is she playing chess instead of engaging in an all-out battle? What's the whole point of this?"

"Balor has to willingly give up his throne. She thought he'd do it once she destroyed his eye. And then she thought he'd do it when she took human hostages. None of those have worked so far." The warrior pressed her lips tightly together. "She's hoping he'll give it up for you."

I stood from the dirt-packed floor and pressed myself up against the bars of the cell. "I don't understand. If she wants it so badly, why hasn't she tried to just take it from him?"

"She can't." The warrior shrugged. "Hell, she tried. And she kept failing. It didn't make a lot of sense until she found out that Balor's throne is protected with a unique kind of magic. So are all the others, actually. Balor has to willingly give up his throne. He can't be killed for it. It's an impossibility."

"And so she's trying to trick him into agreeing to it," I said, frowning. "Just like your friend on the phone."

The warrior's face blanched. "It's best if we don't talk about that."

I raised my eyebrows, edging closer to the bars. "Why not? Your friend is protected by the same magic, right? And she—or he—is going to give up the throne?"

She shifted on her feet and cast a nervous glance over her shoulder at the door. "Nemain will be here any moment now. We shouldn't be talking about this when she arrives."

"Why?" I arched a brow. "Is it because you know she'll kill your friend anyway? As soon as she's officially handed over the throne, Nemain will kill her. You know it's true. She'll never let the previous rulers live. She'll take each and every one of their thrones. And then they'll all be dead."

"Stop it," the warrior said in a hiss. She blinked

rapidly, clearly failing to hold her emotions at bay. I'd hit a nerve. And she hated that I was right.

"Who is it?" I asked in a low whisper. "Just tell me who she's talked into giving up her throne."

"I can't."

The door suddenly swung open behind the warrior. Immediately, her entire body went rigid as she turned to face her Queen. Her whole face was salt white, making her skin look as pale as a corpse. She was terrified of Nemain, and I didn't blame her. Because if she didn't follow her new Queen's orders, she really would look like a corpse. Because she would be one.

"Ah. Thank you, Sophia." Nemain's smile stretched wide across her face as she strode into the dungeons. I dragged my gaze away from the warrior, turning my focus on the female fae I would never call my Queen. She would never have full control over the thrones. She might be out there, and I might be in a cage, but I would never let her get away with it.

"Thank you for stopping by House Futrail, Clark McCann. You've made my mission overwhelmingly easy now."

"It's Cavanaugh," I said through gritted teeth. "And you're going to get a rude awakening when you realise that Balor Beimnech is never going to give up his throne to you."

"That is why *you're* here. Apparently, the human hostages weren't enough, so I had to bring in the big guns. You," she said. "I've delivered my little message to him. Either he gives up his crown and his throne, or you die."

I let out a harsh, bitter laugh. "Balor Beimnech

will never give up his throne, least of all to save me. You do know he banished me, right? You do know that he wants nothing to do with me?"

She pursed her lips. "I was under the impression that he'd welcomed you back into the fold. You've been working with his team, have you not?"

So, Nemain wasn't the all-seeing, all-knowing fae she thought she was.

"Much to his irritation, yes. And our last conversation didn't go so well." I gave her a bitter smile. "Funny, the thing that makes you fail is overestimating Balor's capacity for love. Not sure anyone could have foreseen that coming."

She barked out a laugh, striding toward me and clutching the bars with her perfectly-manicured fingernails. "You're lying. You and Balor have a bond that could never break."

"No. We don't." I fought back the tears. I couldn't let Nemain see me cry, especially not about this. "You saw to that. Remember? As soon as you involved me in your plan to kill his sister, I was dead to him."

It gave me a strange sense of satisfaction to see the look of surprise on her face, even though speaking the words aloud were like a punch in the gut. Balor had kicked me out and turned me away, repeatedly. No matter what I'd done to try and prove my loyalty, he hadn't been able to forget the past. He would not come save me. He would not give up his throne in exchange for my life.

This was the end of the road for me. There was nowhere for me to go, no hope of escaping. It would mean Nemain's failing, yet again, but it would take my life in the process.

27

"You probably shouldn't have told her that Balor's not coming," Sophia said after Nemain had stormed out of the dungeons. Turned out, the warrior fae felt kind of sorry for me. "You could have kept up the act for a little while longer, and she would have kept you alive. Now, she's just going to kill you."

"You say that so matter-of-factly," I replied, pacing from one end of my tiny cell to the other. "I guess it doesn't bother you that she'll just toss me into the sea without a second thought. Along with all the humans she abducted."

Sophia pressed her lips tightly together. "Of course, it bothers me. But she's the Queen. We have to follow her orders, even if we don't like them. That's how these things work."

I scowled and stopped pacing. "That's bullshit, and you know it."

"It's really not. How do you think the Courts have survived this long? It wasn't due to rebels who ignored orders. It was due to falling in line when your Prince or Princess asked it of you."

"It's because of the damn magical bonds, and you know it," I snapped. "Magic. Forcing fae to do things they don't want to do, just because a powerful leader speaks it. Is that what's going on here? Has she created a bond with all the Fianna?"

"Nope," Sophia said. "She can't. Not until she sits on that pile of skulls. Why do you think she needs him to give up his throne willingly? If he doesn't, then she won't have a bond with all his fae."

My eyes widened. "So, that's what all this is about. The magic of the bond won't go to her if she kills him."

"Exactly. She won't fully have them—us—unless he hands it over."

"But that doesn't explain why *you're* doing this," I said, frowning out at her. "You seem like a pretty reasonable fae. No murder eyeballs and all that."

Her lips twitched with a smile she desperately tried to hold back. "Thank you for saying I don't have murder eyeballs."

"You're welcome."

"I just…" She sighed and drifted down the corridor toward me. "I don't really have a choice, Clark. Fionn, and now Aed, pledged their allegiance to Nemain. Them pledging their allegiance meant I had to as well. Otherwise, I would have been banished from the House. They would have sent me away. And I have nothing else. No one else. This House is my life. These warriors are my best friends, my family. From the outside, it's easy to ask why I didn't just walk away, but it's a hell of a lot different when you're inside of it."

"They're your Pack," I said softly.

"Kind of," she said with a slight smile. "I suppose it's not far from the same thing. I've spent my every moment with these fae. I have no idea what my life would be like without them."

I pressed myself up against the bars and gazed out at her. "You do realise that Nemain will not be good for you and your fellow warriors, right? She talks a big game, but it's a bunch of bullshit. When she finally wields her bond over you, she'll make you do anything and everything she wants. And who the hell knows what that'll be?"

She cast a nervous glance over her shoulder. "Look, I understand what you're saying. And I'm not saying I agree or disagree, but the whole situation is a lot more complicated than that. If I went against her now, she'd probably chop my head off."

I gave her a grim smile and nodded. "Yep. She probably would. And you really think that's the right kind of Queen to serve?"

"What is the alternative?" she asked. "And don't say Balor Beimnech. His time as Prince won't last. There are too many fae against him. He's lost his power. He's lost his allies. We need someone else."

My heart hurt hearing the words. Balor was a good Prince. He cared about his people. He'd do anything to protect them, and he had. At the same time, Sophia had some good points. The success of the Courts depended on the happiness of the various Houses that were a part of each Court. While Balor's main base was located in London, he ruled over Houses spread all across Europe.

When those Houses rebelled, he had to deal with it. Luckily, it had been a long time since the fae were involved in serious infighting. Several hundred years ago, things hadn't been quite so peaceful among the Courts. Masters would bicker, even those within the same Court. They backstabbed, broke promises, and even murdered, all in the name of gaining more power and more favour with the Prince.

And when a Prince or Princess could not keep control over his Masters? He was promptly replaced.

Those old ways had died out a long time ago. Most fae just wanted to live peacefully without all the murderous drama that plagued eras past. But if Nemain's recent actions, and those of the Fianna, proved anything, it was that the intense desire for peace was quickly receding.

The fae were beginning to forget what life had once been like, how horrible and brutal all the fighting and wars had been. How terrible the scent of fresh blood was.

With a heavy sigh, I shook my head. "There is no one else. Balor has been the Prince of the Crimson Court for a very long time. He doesn't have any family left to take over for him, and he's not going to hand the reigns over to his second unless he dies."

"Who is his second?"

"That I can't say," I replied. That would be far too much ammunition for Nemain.

A knock sounded on the door. Sophia gave me a weighted glance before she turned and slid open the

ONE FAE IN THE GRAVE

lock. A moment later, Nemain strode into the dungeon with two more Fianna trailing behind her.

She flicked her fingers in my direction. "Pull her out of her cell and take her out onto the lawn. It's time for her execution."

My heart pounded loudly in my ears, and I could barely breathe around the ball of panic in my gut. With wide eyes, I whirled toward Sophia, silently begging for her to do something, anything, whatever it took to stop this thing.

I could tell in her brilliant green eyes that she did not want to watch me die. She might be on the opposite side of this war, but that didn't mean she agreed with everything Nemain said and did. At least for now. As soon as Nemain took over, not that she'd ever convince Balor to give up his throne, she'd transform every single one of the fae's brains to mush. She would control them all. They would be forced to do her every bidding, and she probably wouldn't even let them question it.

They wouldn't be an army of the dead, but they'd be close enough.

Sophia slowly turned toward Nemain as her two fellow warriors quickly surrounded the cell's door. "My Queen. Are you certain she needs to die? She could prove useful to us in the future. Her mind-reading power is quite impressive."

Nemain's glittering eyes narrowed on the female warrior, and a new seed of dread sprouted in my stomach. The Queen, as she had titled herself, did not look pleased that one of her subjects was questioning her in the slightest.

"I have given the order for execution. Do you have a problem with that?" Nemain's voice was full of ice.

Sophia wet her lips. "Not a problem, no." She took a deep breath and turned away, but then her spine suddenly stiffened. "Actually, I do have a problem with it. My Queen. We should keep her here as a prisoner. We don't need to kill her."

"She was spying on us for the enemy. She has conspired against the crown. I gave Balor the choice to save her life, and his decision has been made. He has chosen his throne over Clark's safety. So, she shall die."

Sophia lifted her chin. "Should Clark really be the one to pay for Balor's crimes?"

Nemain spun away from the cell and strode back toward the dungeon exit. She cast a glance over her shoulder at the Fianna warriors, ignoring Sophia. "Bring Clark McCann to the execution block outside. And dispose of the traitor."

Traitor? My eyes widened as the two Fianna spun toward their fellow fae. Sophia had begun to shake her head, backing up to press herself against the crumbling stone wall. All the blood had drained from her face, pulling all the life out of her skin.

"No, you can't." She glanced from one Fianna to the next. "I'm not a traitor. I'd never do anything against the crown. I was just trying to suggest a different option."

"Those with different ideas are not welcome in my Court." Nemain flicked her eyes toward me and smiled. "Anyone who is against me will die."

She pushed out of the dungeon, and the door slammed behind her. I wrapped my hands around the

ONE FAE IN THE GRAVE

steel bars, heart banging hard against my ribcage. I had to do something to stop this. Sophia had only been trying to save my life, and Nemain was going to kill her for it.

But before I could say a word, it was over. One of the Fianna drew his dagger and sliced it across Sophia's neck. She didn't have time to react. There were no last words. One moment, she was here, and the next she was gone.

Horror filled my gut as the blood sprayed across the stone walls. Her body crumpled to the ground, legs and arms cruelly twisted. Her eyes were open wide, full of fear and shock. I pressed my hand to my mouth and swallowed down the churning in my gut.

How could Nemain have done this? How could she have so coldly murdered one of her own?

The Fianna who had swung the blade now ripped my cell door open. I had no choice but to stand silently while he tightened magical chains around my wrists and my ankles, to keep me from transforming back into my bird.

He jerked on my chain, pulling me toward the door that would lead me to my death. My boots scuffed through blood as we passed Sophia's broken body, and the shifter inside of me itched to get out.

I was being led to my death. And they'd rendered my magic useless.

Balor hadn't come. Just like I'd known he wouldn't. He'd made his feelings for me more than clear. He considered me the enemy. Someone he hated. Someone who didn't deserve to live.

When the door opened, a large figured hurtled into the dungeons. Everything happened so fast that it took my mind some time to catch up. There was a blur of bodies, shouts peppering the air, and the sound of steel slicing through the air. Blood soared through the air in an arc as the steel made contact with the Fianna's head.

I turned toward the attacker, heart hammering so hard my entire body shook.

Balor stood before me, his body heaving, his single visible eye so alight with anger that I had to take a step back.

"You're here," I whispered. "You came."

"I was always going to come for you, Clark. Now, get behind me."

28

Balor quickly dispatched the second Fianna. It only took a single slash of his sword, and our enemy was sprawled on the ground with thick blood oozing from his neck. My heart hammered hard as I watched Balor wipe the gore from the blade. He was here. He'd come for me. After all that had happened for him to push me away, he'd still come to save me from this place.

"Balor," I said softly.

Slowly, he turned to face me, his entire body tense. The threat was gone now, but he didn't look pleased. His face was all hard lines and furrowed brows.

"Hello, Clark." He reached out a hand and cupped my cheek, the hardness in his eyes softening for just a moment. "I'm so glad you're okay."

"You came for me. I…"

"You didn't think I would." A flicker of pain crossed his face. "Of course you wouldn't. I've done nothing to convince you otherwise these past few weeks. I've pushed you away. I've done everything I could to block you out of my life."

"You shouldn't have, you know." My voice cracked on the last syllable. "I understand why you pushed me away at first, but then after everything that happened…"

A tear slipped down my cheek. The last thing I wanted to do was break down in front of Balor, even though he'd just saved me from the Fianna. I wanted him to apologise. I wanted him to admit that I was not the kind of fae he'd been accusing me of being. He knew the truth of my step-father. He knew I'd been manipulated. As horrible as the whole thing had been, he couldn't keep holding that against me. Not if we were ever going to get back to where we used to be.

Sadness filled his eye, his finger sliding down my cheek to catch the tear. He took a step closer to me, pulling me tight against his body. Everything within me clenched tight, regardless of all the hurt and pain I'd felt these past few weeks. The warmth of him, the feel of him, it chased all those feelings away.

"Clark," he said, voice rough with emotion. "I am so sorry. When I found out Nemain had you here, I realised I couldn't keep pretending to hold a grudge I shouldn't even have. Fuck what everyone else thinks. I want you by my side, Clark. You're the most important thing in my life. I don't care what happened ten years ago. All I care is what happens now. With you. And me."

My heart pulsed in my chest. Tears filled my eyes as I stared up at Balor, drinking in his face. All the steel and ice were gone once again. The truth of him was standing right in front of me, and he was asking me to forgive him.

He had hurt me. That much was true. But I had also hurt him by keeping the truth hidden all those weeks. Things might have gone differently if I'd been up front, if I'd been the one to tell him first. We'd both been wrong. We'd both made mistakes. I could either forgive him now, or I could walk away from him and the Court forever.

I pressed my hands against his chest and breathed him in. "I couldn't stay angry with you, even if I wanted to."

It was the truth. No matter what happened, I couldn't get Balor Beimnech out of my head. It wasn't his allure. I knew that now. He didn't even have that damn power. It was something else. Something I couldn't ignore. A bond had formed between us, and it had nothing to do with his status as a Prince.

It went much deeper than that.

"Oh, Clark." His head dipped low, and his lips brushed against mine. My entire body sparked with life. I leaned into the kiss, opening my mouth wider, need filling my gut.

His touch made me sigh, as if I'd been holding my breath all these weeks we'd spent apart. Now, I could breathe again. Now, I could be whole. A piece of me had been missing while we'd been apart, and it slid into place as his mouth caressed mine and his hands roamed across my body.

A need exploded from my core. Moaning, I laced my hands around the back of his neck and pressed up onto my toes, desperate for more. Balor growled in response, his own hands snaking around my body. He lifted me from the floor, carried me across the corridor, and slammed me back against the wall.

I twisted my hands in his silver-streaked hair, pulling him closer to me as I clung tight to his waist with my thighs. God, I needed him. More than I'd needed anything in my life.

Slowly, Balor paused and pulled back to stare deeply into my eyes. His chest was heaving; his cheeks were flushed with red. "Clark. Are you sure you want to do this?"

My heart pounded hard. "Kiss you? Hell yes, I'm sure."

I'd never been more sure of anything in my life.

He gave his head a quick shake. "I mean, me and you. Us. Our coupling. Are you sure you want to do this? It will change everything. Our lives and the Court will never be the same after this."

"Coupling," I repeated dumbly. "You don't mean…?"

I trailed off, not daring to speak the word out loud. *Coupling* (well, true coupling anyway) was totally off-limits when it came to me and Balor. There was that whole pesky prophecy, the one that said Balor's offspring would one day be the very thing that destroyed him and his Court. He'd pushed me away time and time again for this very reason. We couldn't be intimate, and we knew we couldn't control ourselves if we gave in to how we felt.

What had changed? Did he no longer believe the prophecy was real?

I wasn't sure it was a risk I was willing to take.

"I mean exactly what I said," he said in a low growl. His hand pressed firmly against my back, shooting new waves of warmth into my body. I sighed and leaned into him, desperately wanting to give in to what I'd been yearning for all this time.

Instead, I unhooked my legs, sucked a deep breath in through my nose, and stepped back. "The prophecy."

His eye flickered with desire. "We can find a way to work around the prophecy. There are ways to avoid my seed getting inside of you while still giving in to what we want. You do still want that from me, Clark?"

I did. I wanted nothing more.

Breathing in the scent of him, I pressed up onto my toes and took his mouth in mine. He kissed me deeply, his hands roaming across every inch of my back. I clung on tight, half-fearing that if I let go then I'd never again have the chance to hold him close.

A deep, warm sense of satisfaction spread through my body. Where our lips touched, where his hand was on my skin, magic pulsed. That same strange magic I felt anytime I was near him. For the longest time, I'd thought it was his allure, a power he had over every female—or male—he met. Nothing about how he made me feel was normal. It came with a power that sucked every breath from my lungs.

When I finally pulled away from him, he was smiling. It had been a long time since I'd seen that kind of expression on his face. "What is this, Balor? What's happening between us?"

He shook his head, cupped my cheek. "To be honest, I've never experienced anything like this before. But, if I had to guess, Clark, I'd say the magic that pulses between us, the impossible-to-ignore bond we share…it means that we're mates."

I sucked in a sharp breath.

Mates.

Caer had insinuated the possibility we were mates from my very first day in the Crimson Court. She'd said our futures were entwined. I'd tried to come up with explanation after explanation for what that meant.

But the most logical explanation was that we were mates, something that rarely happened in the current Faerie world. In the past, mates had been as regular as the changing seasons. Males and females, or males and males, or females and females, joined together based on an unbreakable bond created by magic.

That was then, and this was now. And now… bonds were not very common.

"So, we're mates," I breathed, staring up at him.

He smiled down at me. "We're mates."

An explosion shook the dungeon floor, breaking through the moment. Clinging to each other, we turned toward the open door and stared out at the dim corridor. The sound of pounding feet drifted toward us. Something was happening. People were coming. Nemain had no doubt been informed that Balor had come.

My Prince and I took one look at each other, clasped hands, and charged out the door.

29

*B*alor and I strode out of the dungeon. I didn't have my sword, so he kept his body just in front of mine, blocking me from the impending attackers. There were at least two dozen Fianna on the premises, not to mention all of the other fae who called this House their home.

We were greatly outnumbered, and Balor no longer held the power of his eye. If we wanted to make it out of here alive, we needed to move quickly.

After turning corridor after corridor, I spotted the side door down an adjacent hallway. We spun around the corner, hands linked. Only to come face-to-face with Nemain.

She stood in the center of the hallway, her arms crossed over her chest, perfectly-manicured fingernails tapping in rhythm with our footsteps. "Leaving so soon? I'm surprised you haven't made an attempt to free the human hostages."

The human hostages. In the thrill of seeing Balor, I had forgotten about all of the humans Nemain had taken prisoner in hopes of tricking Balor into giving up his throne.

"You killed them, Nemain," he said in a low, dangerous voice. "I saw the bodies outside with my own eyes."

Pain lanced through my heart. All those human lives, lost because Nemain was desperate for power.

"*Eye*," she said with a grin. "Singular. You have just the one now, though I have to say the eye patch still looks handsome on that chiseled face of yours."

Irritation ripped through my gut. "Get out of our way. Now. You may have taken Balor's power away from him, but he's still the strongest fighter I've ever met."

"Oh, I'm certain he is," she said with a tinkling laugh. "And I don't want to fight him, hence the lack of Fianna in this corridor. However, I am not just going to step aside. Nor will you want me to."

Balor shifted closer to her, his hands tight around the golden hilt of his sword. "What is it that you want, Nemain? You want me to give up my throne? It's not going to happen. I will never step aside, not when you're out in the world trying to take control of all of Faerie."

With that, she laughed. A loud, booming sound that filled up the corridor. It held so much darkness, so much danger, that it made me take a step back. Until now, she'd done nothing but speak in cooing tones, and laugh in a way that sounded like bells.

But the true depths of her darkness was coming out of her now. And it was terrifying.

"You are going to change your mind when you hear what I want to propose," she said.

I shot a glance at Balor. "We should just go. Whatever she has to say, it won't be good. Let's get out of here now and go home."

Home to my Court. Home to my friends. It was an ache inside of me, one that could only be filled when I was finally back where I needed to be. And I was terrified that whatever Nemain said now would mean I would never again walk through those doors.

"It is my duty to hear what she has to say," Balor finally said, though he didn't loosen the grip on his sword. "But make it quick, Nemain. I won't hesitate to slash you to shreds."

"I have the Bullaun," she said quickly, perhaps realising just how serious Balor was. "The cursing stone. The one I used to fate every single fae in your House to die."

Balor went still, and the hallway grew so quiet that I swore I could hear the spiders scrabbling around in the dark corners. "That is not exactly new information, Nemain."

"But what is new information is that it is here, right inside this House." She gestured at the hallway behind her. "You could search for it, if you want, but you won't find it. You need me to give it to you."

"And I suppose you're just going to hand it over, are you?" I couldn't help but snap before turning to Balor. "Come on. She's just trying to bait us into doing something we're both going to regret. We need to leave, Balor."

"What do you want for the stone?" he asked Nemain, inching a step closer to her.

Her smile widened. "I want your fucking throne."

A long, horrible moment stretched out before us.

My heart thumped hard against my ribcage, pulsing with a kind of dread that terrified me. I knew without looking at Balor's face that Nemain had caught him in her snare. Balor would never give up his throne. Not for some human hostages. Not for some other promise of power. But when it came to the lives of his faithful fae, he would do anything.

He had spent his entire life protecting them. He'd lied to the world, built himself up to be a monster he was not. All to scare everyone else off, all to keep them safe. But Nemain could not be scared. Her greed for power was far too great; her need for blood far too terrible.

"Be very clear in what you are offering me," Balor said quietly, lowering his sword to his side. "You will give me the Bullaun, the one that will undo the curse. In return, you want me to give up my throne. Do I have that right?"

"That is exactly what I am proposing." The smile fell from her face. She was nothing but pure fire now, the seriousness of her deal reflected in the dark pools of her eyes. "Your throne for the lives of your people. What will it be, Balor the smiter?"

My heart banged hard in my chest. He was going to do it. He was going to give it all up for the lives of everyone he loved. I opened my mouth to try and stop him from turning his entire life upside down, but I couldn't do it.

This was the only way to save them. The only way to make sure they didn't die gruesome deaths. Balor had filled me in while we'd been running through the halls. We'd already lost Cormac to this, and several more fae had passed in the past twenty-four hours. If

Balor didn't accept this deal, I knew Nemain would never back down. She would let the curse play out, killing every last fae in Balor's House.

Finally, Balor gave a nod, his voice raw when he spoke. "It's a deal. You will give me the Bullaun, and I will give you my throne."

Nemain's eyes lit up with pure delight. She clapped her hands, magic swarming through the hallway. It curled around her, picking up the strands of her long dark hair. She rose from the ground, her hands held high by her sides. She looked like some kind of avenging demon, her skin glowing red.

"I hid the stone in Clark's cell," Nemain said, her voice hollow and full of an eerie power that made every hair on my arms stand on end. "Go now before I decide to kill you both."

30

*B*alor and I placed the cursing stone on the slab of rock that Duncan, Moira, Ronan, and I had found in the Irish forest. It fit perfectly in the groove, filling up the indentation as if it had been carved specifically for this spot.

"Looks like she wasn't lying," I said, taking a step back from the stone platform. "She took the Bullaun from here."

"Yes. One of the few truths Nemain has ever said." The space between Balor's eyes was pinched. It had been like that from the moment we'd grabbed the rock and fled. I knew he wanted to go back and try to take her down, but he had willingly given up his throne to her. There was no way to undo that now, not even with her death. Her status as Princess of the Crimson Court would now be protected just like his had.

On the way out of the House, we'd put the call in to Moira and Elise, to warn them about what was coming for them. They would try to evacuate as many fae as possible, though not everyone would make it out. Moira had looked out the window and had spotted dozens upon dozens of Fianna surrounding the place. Clearly, Nemain had left them in London, just waiting for the right moment.

"You should be the one to do it," I said to Balor, nodding at the stone. "You gave up everything for their lives."

Balor's jaw rippled as he stared straight ahead, as if he were looking into the depths of nothingness. For a moment, I thought he would refuse, that he'd decide to step back away from the stones.

But, of course, he could never walk away from this. These were his people, even if they now belonged to someone else. With a deep breath, he stepped up to the platform and wrapped his trembling hands around the rock. His shoulders shook as he stared down at it, as he muttered words too low for me to hear.

And then he began to turn the stone, twisting it to undo the curse. The sky overhead crackled as wind swept through the forest clearing. The trees bent sideways, the top branches scratching against the dirt-packed ground. I gritted my teeth against the force of the magic charging around us. It was electric and fierce, far stronger than any magic I'd experienced until now.

Except maybe my battle cry.

An idea popped into my head as Balor finished off the spell. His breath was ragged as he stepped away, and he wiped a dash of sweat off his brow.

He gave me a nod. "That was it. The curse is over. The fae of House Beimnech are saved, though I suppose the name of the House will now change."

"You saved them." I slid my hand into his and gazed up at him, my heart swelling so large with the love I felt.

"I saved their lives. But I've doomed them to something else. Nothing will ever be the same for them after this, and I shudder to think of what will happen to the vampires. Hopefully, the Pack truly did get out before the Fianna swarmed through the streets."

"Well, I have an idea," I said in a small voice. I was almost afraid to speak it out loud for how crazy it sounded even inside my own head. Obviously, I was not the Morrigan, but…I had some kind of power. One that made enemies drop dead in their tracks. I didn't truly understand it yet, nor did I know how to control it. But it was there.

He lifted a brow. "Why do I have the feeling I'm not going to like this idea of yours?"

I cracked a grin. "Probably because you're never a big fan of most of my ideas."

"You're not wrong about that." He let out a heavy sigh. "Well, go on then, let's hear it. Before I change my mind."

"We're going to take back your Court, and we're going to make sure that Nemain doesn't sit her ass on a throne ever again."

"And you have a plan for this impossible mission of yours, I'm presuming?"

"We're going to figure out what the hell is going on with my…well, you called it a battle cry, so let's go with that. And then we're going to use it to take down Nemain and her army."

"She will have inherited the same protection that I

once had." Balor frowned. "If we kill her, we can't get the throne back. The only way I was able to stop Fionn was because of the nature of his rebellion. He crept his way in there, called Faerie. I willingly backed down to Nemain. It's hers now."

Balor wasn't going to like the next words that were going to come out of my mouth. He was a lot older than I was; his world was Faerie and the rules and customs that went along with it. But it was the only way that I could see this ending once and for all.

"Maybe it wouldn't be such a bad thing for no one to sit on the throne, for there to be no more bonds." I slid my hand into his and squeezed tight. "And if no one sits on that throne, Balor, Caer's prophecy will no longer count."

～

Thank you for reading *One Fae in the Grave*! Book 5 in the Paranormal PI Files will be launching at the end of July. You can sign up to my reader newsletter to be notified on release day.

ABOUT THE AUTHOR

Jenna Wolfhart is a Buffy-wannabe who lives vicariously through the kick-ass heroines in urban fantasy. After completing a PhD in Librarianship, she became a full-time author and now spends her days typing the fantastical stories in her head. When she's not writing, she loves to stargaze, rewatch Game of Thrones, and drink copious amounts of coffee.

Born and raised in America, Jenna now lives in England with her husband, her dog, and her mischief of rats.

FIND ME ONLINE
Facebook Reader Group
Instagram
YouTube
Twitter

www.jennawolfhart.com
jenna@jennawolfhart.com

Printed in Great Britain
by Amazon